Twenty-four hours

In twenty-four hours she'd insulted Kevin, told him off, listened as he told her off, eaten two meals with this man, completely lost her mind out on a rainy stretch of highway, let him go to the local mall to buy her clothing, gone swimming and into the Jacuzzi with him....

And wanted him to kiss her.

And kissed him.

Twenty-four hours.

This can't be happening to me....

ABOUT THE AUTHOR

Elda Minger became a writer via a circuitous route. Through the years she has worked in several bookstores, cleaned houses in Beverly Hills, ushered in theaters, sung for her supper on Hollywood Boulevard and even appeared in two movies. Born in and now residing again in Hollywood, California, Elda has lived in many parts of the United States, as well as in many foreign countries, including Italy.

Books by Elda Minger
HARLEQUIN AMERICAN ROMANCE

Don't miss any of our special offers. Write to us at the following address for information on our newest releases.

Harlequin Reader Service
901 Fuhrmann Blvd., P.O. Box 1397, Buffalo, NY 14240
Canadian address: P.O. Box 603,
Fort Erie, Ont. L2A 5X3

SPIKE
IS
MISSING

ELDA MINGER

Harlequin Books

TORONTO • NEW YORK • LONDON
AMSTERDAM • PARIS • SYDNEY • HAMBURG
STOCKHOLM • ATHENS • TOKYO • MILAN

Published April 1990

First printing February 1990

ISBN 0-373-16338-X

Chapter One

"Spike is missing."

"Oh, very funny." Gillian Sommers's voice was muffled. She was on her knees, her head beneath her desk, trying to retrieve the piece of gourmet chocolate-chip cookie that had fallen on the carpeted floor.

"I'm serious, Sommers. Spike is missing."

All action beneath the desk stilled, then Gillian hauled herself up, knowing she looked less than dignified. But who cared about dignified? If Spike *was* missing, the prize client's spokescat wouldn't be available for filming.

"Since when?"

"Last night. He didn't come home." The bearer of this bad news was Corbin Spencer. Tall, blue-eyed, blond and ambitious, Corbin could be counted on to always have his ear to the office door. Gillian had found him an invaluable associate when she needed to know if a vital piece of office gossip was true.

"All cats stray."

"The compound is entirely fenced in. There's not a chance in the world he could have slipped out. Besides, his trainer told Ben he's always on time for dinner—as long as it isn't Kitty Krunchies. That fat cat hasn't missed a meal in five years.''

Ben knows. Spike is missing. We're all doomed.

The Merrill Advertising Agency was one of the most prestigious in Los Angeles, and for good reason. They had a reputation for being able to persuade even the most jaded consumer into buying just about anything.

And what they had done for the Kitty Krunchies Kat Food Company had been truly outstanding. Three years ago, when the company had approached them, their product had been going down the tubes fast. With the help of some of the best writers in the business and the addition of Spike as a Morrislike representative of the "new and improved" Kitty Krunchies Kat Food, sales had skyrocketed.

A new series of commercials, starring Spike, was scheduled to shoot at the end of the month. The Kitty Krunchies Kat Food Company was one of Merrill's biggest accounts. Gillian grasped the edge of her desk as Corbin's information began to sink in.

No cat, no commercials. No commercials, no account. Lose that account, heads roll.

She had brought in that account, it was her baby. Now she had to get as much information as possible before Ben called her into his office. She had to be on top of things, look as efficient and cool as she usually did.

Think fast.

"What's the name of that trainer?"

"Kevin MacClaine."

"Where's Ben?"

"He went out to lunch, but he should be back in about ten minutes."

"Get out of here, I've got calls to make."

Even as Corbin left, Gillian's fingers were flying to her Rolodex. *MacArdle, MacArthur—MacClaine.* As she dialed, she tried to conjure up his face. She'd met him once at a bash thrown by Kitty Krunchies. He was cute, if you liked that windblown, outdoorsy type, all muscles and tanned skin.

He had freckles, she remembered suddenly. *And blue, blue eyes.* And his phone kept ringing and ringing.

No one home.

She hung up the phone, then glanced at the clock. Seven minutes to go, and her boss, Ben Merrill, would walk in the door and ask to see her in his office.

And she had absolutely no idea what she was going to tell him.

KEVIN MACCLAINE LAY in a hammock under a willow tree at the far end of his animal compound. He'd placed the stakes supporting the hammock beneath this tree for a very specific reason. When one lived on a compound with various animals, there were times when you desperately needed a little privacy.

He needed time to think.

Spike, where are you?

The last time he'd seen the massive tabby, Spike had been stretched out on his bed, lying on an afghan. He'd staked out a patch of sunshine. Five years old, thirty-two pounds, a ripped ear and a scarred face,

Spike was an original, and perhaps his favorite animal. The cat had a personality that just didn't quit.

Ever since Kevin had brought him to the compound Spike had seemed content. He hadn't strayed before. He'd seemed content with the slow, lazy pace.

But now he was gone.

It doesn't make sense. Why would Spike leave? The compound was cat nirvana. Plenty of room, good food, never a dull moment. And love. Kevin loved all his animals, cared for them as carefully as he did his nieces and nephews when they came to visit him. He considered each of his animal's specific personality, needs and wants.

Spike hadn't seemed restless.

Kevin stretched, then sighed, knowing he'd have to start evening feedings soon. And knowing he was no closer to figuring out this entire mess.

He wasn't worried so much about the series of commercials scheduled for the end of the month. All his concern was for Spike. The Greater Los Angeles Basin could be a harsh place for a lost animal.

He'd certainly rescued enough of them.

He'd have to call her soon. Kevin closed his eyes as he tried to visualize her, remember her name. The woman at the agency who had picked Spike. Jenny? No. Janet?

Coppery hair, green eyes, slim figure. Cute, if you didn't mind the tight-assed way she dressed. And he had. When they had been introduced at a Kitty Krunchies party, she'd held out her hand politely, but the expression in her eyes had made it very clear she considered him to be another windblown jock, an athletic moron.

He wondered suddenly why what she'd thought of him mattered at all.

Gillian. Gillian Sommers. He had a good memory; it just took a little while for it to kick into gear.

He glanced at his watch. One-thirty. She was probably at lunch. He'd go inside around three and give her a call.

"I DON'T HAVE TO TELL YOU what will happen if we can't find that cat by the time they're ready to shoot the next series of commercials."

Gillian merely looked at Ben, understanding in her eyes. Ben Merrill had brought the agency up single-handedly. In his early fifties, he had a long, lean build and the fastest mind she'd ever observed. Ben had been her mentor from the time she had started working at the Merrill Agency.

"We've got to find that cat. Have you talked to his trainer?"

"I tried calling him just a few minutes ago. No one answered the phone."

"Damn. Maybe you should drive out there tonight. Do you remember where the place is?"

"I can find it." Gillian prided herself on her ability to use maps. She rarely got lost.

"Good. I'd say we don't have much time to lose. Especially since the damn cat has never turned up missing at dinnertime before this."

BIRDY'S LEGS WERE TIRED. It was only a quarter mile to the local Von's Market, but today, on the way back home, she was feeling every step. Her daughter had sent her a generous check this month, which she'd put to good use buying groceries.

But Birdy would have much preferred time with her daughter to the money she regularly sent her.

She suspected Diana was guilty. Guilty because she didn't really want to spend much time with her mother. There was a peculiar pain in raising a daughter who had been so delightful as a little girl but who had grown up to be ashamed of you.

And Birdy knew her daughter was ashamed of her. Ashamed of the fact that she still lived in the cluttered, one-bedroom apartment in Panorama City. Ashamed that she wouldn't—*couldn't*—grow old gracefully and simply fade into the woodwork.

Oh, she knew her daughter still loved her. This had nothing to do with love, it was more painful than that. The mother-daughter bond would never be broken, but Diana didn't really like her. When Diana entered her teen years, the eccentricities that had been fun when she was a little girl became painfully embarrassing.

Now, while Birdy lived in the San Fernando Valley outside the city of Los Angeles, Diana lived on the East Coast. A suburb outside of Philadelphia. She'd married a very wealthy man. She sent checks to her mother regularly. And Birdy needed the money, because living on a fixed income wasn't easy.

She still missed her daughter.

Birdy sighed as she pulled the small metal grocery cart behind her. Michael Sullivan, ten years old and her best friend on the block, had promised to come by and help her with her grocery shopping. They made a strange pair, the old woman in her sixties and the young boy, but they understood each other.

Both, in their own ways, were outcasts.

She stopped at the corner, let go of the cart for an instant and rubbed her fingers together. Sometimes, when the temperature dropped unexpectedly, her bones hurt. Arthritis had plagued her since she was in her thirties, and she knew exactly what to do to keep it from hurting.

But groceries had to be bought. Life still had to go on. Birdy wasn't a pessimistic woman by nature, but lately life had become a little more lonely than she would have liked it to be.

The meow was so very soft she wouldn't have heard it if there had been heavy traffic in the street.

As it was, she still wasn't sure what she'd heard or where it was coming from. Birdy cocked her head and everything within her stilled as she concentrated on listening.

I'm imagining things.

No, there it was again. The tiniest little squeak, like the kittens she had found in a bag under a freeway overpass. She had taken all five of them home, bottle-fed them until they could eat solid food, then found each of them a home.

Birdy's one luxury in life was her weekly bingo game at the local Catholic church. She sat at a specific table up front with her friends. Each of those friends had sons and daughters, husbands, nieces and nephews. Plenty of people who wanted a kitten or knew someone who did.

Another kitten. People's cruelty had stopped surprising her some years ago. She couldn't prevent any of it, but she could respond. Now Birdy did what she had to. And that included leaving her cart at the corner and following the small sound.

The lot on the corner was empty, overrun with weeds and litter. Thick bushes separated the lot from the tall, pink stucco apartment building next to it.

She heard the sound again, a plaintive little meow that tore at her heart. She was closer now. Birdy knelt and shielded her eyes against the bright California sun.

It took her a minute to see beneath the tangle of bushes, but slowly a large cat came into focus. He was a gray tabby, lying on his side. His fur was matted, but it was his back leg, twisted up the way it was, that caught Birdy's eye immediately.

Broken.

The animal was lying in the cool dirt, its breathing shallow, just the tip of its pink tongue showing at its mouth. The cat opened its mouth, and another of the soft meows broke the silence.

Birdy glanced back at her cart. A week and a half's worth of groceries lay in that cart, along with most of her money for the month. But she didn't hesitate as she walked back toward the cart, then slowly pulled it toward the bushes. Birdy carefully lifted out two bags of groceries, then took off her sweater and made a soft resting place at the bottom of the cart.

Getting the cat out from under the bushes was going to be tricky.

She was down on her hands and knees when she heard Michael.

"Hey, Birdy! What're you doing?"

She glanced back. Michael was still a few houses down, but he was running energetically toward her. Towheaded, blue-eyed, in his usual uniform of jeans and a T-shirt, he was a most welcome sight.

"Michael," she said quietly as the boy reached her side, "there's an injured cat underneath that bush and we have to get him out."

"Okay." Birdy knew Michael was used to her animal rescues by now; he had helped her care for so many of the strays she had taken in. She had never questioned him as to why he spent so little time at home and so much time with her, but she guessed he was lonely. And perhaps had a need to be needed.

"I can crawl under the bush and get him."

"We can't move him much. I think his leg is twisted. Wait a minute, Michael, let me think." As Birdy wondered what they were going to do, her gaze fell on some of the trash at the far end of the lot.

"Michael, could you get me that cardboard box?"

"Sure."

Within fifteen minutes the box had been flattened, and Michael was on his stomach next to the bushes, easing the cardboard beneath the large cat.

"Easy, Michael. We don't want to hurt him any more than we have to." Birdy watched the animal carefully, not wanting Michael to get scratched. The tomcat didn't resist being moved at all, and that told her just how much pain the animal was in.

"Let's get him to the vet's."

"What about your stuff?"

Birdy thought quickly. "Michael, if you can just get out the eggs and the milk, we can slide the rest of it underneath the bushes and come back later."

Michael's eyes lit up at this. "I can help you. I'll come back with my bike and get it for you."

"That would be wonderful, dear."

THIS GUY LIVES at the end of the world.

Gillian consulted her map again, then folded it and, glancing back, pulled away from the curb. She felt completely out of place this far out in the valley. It was about as far as one could get from Century City, with its high-rises, ultraefficient offices and trendy restaurants. This part of the Los Angeles Basin was still rough and tumble, zoned for horses, more primitive.

She tried to picture Kevin again and could only remember his eyes. Blue, so very blue. They'd been alive, lit with mischief. She remembered thinking that although he hadn't seemed out of place at the Kitty Krunchies party, she had sensed he thought the entire thing was a little ridiculous.

She hadn't liked that. Gillian didn't particularly like people who made fun of what she did. She knew advertising wasn't something that was going to save the world, but it certainly had its place in the scheme of things.

Turn left here.

She handled her dark gray BMW with the expertise of someone who enjoyed driving and did a lot of it. The car had been her gift to herself after a particularly successful year with the firm. She'd been thinking of something a little less flashy, less expensive. But Corbin had gone shopping with her and somewhere along the line had implied he thought she wouldn't be able to afford this particular car. That and the fact that Gillian had fallen in love with the way the BMW handled had sealed her fate.

She parked the car at the address she had written down from her Rolodex, then got out and stretched. It had been a long drive, the traffic made more bearable by the efficient air conditioning and Sting's singing on her tape cassette.

Now, on to Kevin MacClaine.

She could barely see the house. Thick foliage obscured the lot from the quiet street. It was a large lot, stretching down most of the long block, and she couldn't see where it ended.

Gillian was just coming up to the chain-link fence when she heard something scream. Some kind of bird. A dog barked, then another, and as she came to the gate she saw five pairs of canine eyes staring at her, all extremely curious.

They made a comical grouping. Gillian didn't know much about dogs, so she could only guess at what they were. A large black dog looked at her with a suspicious expression in his dark eyes. Racing around below him were three other dogs. They had to be mutts, because they didn't look like any dogs she had ever seen. Bushy hair, airplane ears and large, ungainly paws. The last dog seemed almost shy and looked a little like Lassie.

She stepped closer to the gate and the big, dark dog gave a low growl. The three bushy-haired dogs began to bark furiously and the shy dog wheeled and bolted.

If Kevin MacClaine was home, then this racket would bring him outside quickly.

She only had to stand there for another minute before he appeared.

"Gillian?"

She couldn't fathom the look on his face. It was part resignation, part apprehension. Yet he wasn't flustered at all.

He wasn't completely dressed, either.

The only thing he wore was a pair of threadbare denim cutoffs. They rode low on his lean hips. His chest was bare, and she noticed that the muscles in his shoulders and abdomen were clearly defined, almost sculpted. And she thought about the men she knew in Century City who went to the gym religiously every lunch hour in order to achieve such a body.

She had a feeling that this man didn't patronize any expensive health club.

"Gillian?" He spoke again, and she realized she was staring.

Quickly she regained her composure, years of company experience coming quickly to the fore. "Yes. You must be Kevin."

He smiled then, slowly, and she remembered that devilish grin from the party. He'd grinned when they had unveiled the new Kitty Krunchies packaging, and that grin had seemed to say he could barely restrain his laughter.

This grin was different. It was genuine, and she was suddenly reminded of the boy that had lived next door to her when she had been small. He had come to her house every day asking if she or her brothers could play. That grin had promised lots of fun and adventures.

It had been cute on that boy. It was absolutely devastating on this man.

"Come on in. Bruno, down!"

Though she didn't have any pets of her own, except an overweight goldfish, Gillian wasn't afraid of animals. When Kevin opened the chain-link gate, she slipped inside. Instantly she was surrounded by four sniffing noses.

"Leave the lady alone and keep your noses to yourselves." There was a hint of laughter in his voice. The dogs, seemingly satisfied with her, bounded on ahead, except for the smallest of the bushy mutts. She stayed at Kevin's side.

"You've come about Spike."

Gillian had to admire the man. He didn't waste time.

"Yes. When was the last time you saw him?"

"Two days ago, lying on my bed. Spike's pretty predictable, he's always on time for meals, and he doesn't stray. When he didn't show up for dinner, I wasn't that worried. When he wasn't around for breakfast, I called the agency."

So that was how Ben had found out. And as Corbin had his ear constantly pressed to the main man's office door, he had found out as soon as Ben had.

Kevin was leading the way up a short flight of steps. The stucco house was large and airy, and as they entered the front door, she could hear more of the screaming she had heard from the gate.

"This way. Would you like something to drink?"

Even with air conditioning, the drive out had been a long one.

"Yes."

"Coke, orange juice, coffee—"

"Coke's fine."

The kitchen was large, cool and very clean. There was a Dutch door that led to a large room in back, then another door at the end of that room that led directly outside. The faint smell of antiseptic was in the air, and Gillian's questioning look must have made sense to Kevin.

"Clementine the pig cut herself. The vet was out here this morning."

She nodded as if this made perfect sense, then accepted the can of Coke he handed her.

"Right this way. We can talk in here."

Here turned out to be a breakfast nook. The small room looked out over the front of the compound. As Gillian sat down, she tried not to stare at the three enormous perches also in the room. Their occupants were equally flamboyant.

The parrots were brilliantly feathered, their eyes sharp and intelligent.

"Hi, honey!" This came out of the mouth of a green-and-yellow bird. He began to stroll down his perch in her direction, and Gillian shifted ever so slightly on her seat so that he couldn't reach her.

"He won't hurt you. Harpo's just a big ham."

"What a good little Harpo!" Harpo shouted in answer, and Gillian had to smile.

The fuzzy mutt still at Kevin's feet barked sharply, and Harpo retorted, "Shut that flea bag up!"

She turned to Kevin, her mouth open. "He can really talk!"

"Parrots are pretty intelligent."

The other large bird was a mixture of brilliant scarlets, yellows and blues. The third was smaller than the other two and a vivid green.

"This one seems kind of shy."

"She's new. C'mere Jade, c'mon baby." As he spoke, Kevin offered the smaller parrot his hand. The bird hesitated slightly, then stepped up onto his fingers. Gillian watched as Kevin slowly moved his hand, and the bird stepped onto his shoulder.

"Want a kiss?" Harpo asked.

"No thanks," Gillian replied without thinking.

"What a beautiful bird!" Harpo said, his eyes bright.

When Gillian glanced back at Kevin, he was smiling at her.

Jade was brushing up against him; it seemed she was cuddling up to Kevin.

"I didn't know they were that affectionate."

"It depends on the bird. They all have different personalities."

"How about a pizza?" Harpo asked, eyeing Kevin hopefully.

"Not tonight, sport. You're getting to be a real pig."

Harpo merely laughed.

Gillian took a sip of her Coke. For a minute, watching Kevin with all his animals, she'd forgotten why she was here. It wasn't often that she forgot her work and she was surprised at herself. But the thought of Ben back at the office and the meeting she would be having with him early the next morning prompted her next question.

"Spike is due to start shooting the new series of Kitty Krunchies commercials—"

"I know. But right now I'm just a little more worried about Spike than the commercials."

"Of course." She was suddenly ashamed of the way she'd sounded, worried about the agency and their account and unconcerned about Spike.

"I didn't mean to sound that way. Of course you're worried about your cat."

The look in his eyes was unfathomable. "Thanks."

There was an uncomfortable pause, then Kevin came straight to the point. "Just why exactly are you here?"

"Ben asked me to come out and talk to you. Find out firsthand what happened. I'm supposed to report back to him in the morning."

"Hmm. I've told you everything I know. Spike's usually around the compound. One minute he was lying in the sun, the next he was late for dinner."

"Has he ever run away before?"

The smile was completely off his face, out of his eyes, when he looked at her. "I don't think he ran away."

She wasn't following his train of thought. "If he didn't run away, then where is he?"

Kevin glanced away from her then took a deep breath. He looked her directly in the eye. "I think someone stole him."

"What?"

"Specifically, someone who might have something to gain. Spike's contract was up for renegotiation. There was no question about what I was going to do. He's making so much money for Kitty Krunchies, I thought it was about time he saw a little more of it. I guess someone didn't want that to happen."

"Oh, I can't believe this! You think someone in the agency *deliberately* snuck onto your property and stole Spike off your bed? How could they have gotten past all the dogs?"

"Stranger things have been known to happen when money's involved."

He was perfectly calm, and somehow that calm was beginning to infuriate her.

"Give me a break." In the back of her mind Gillian realized she was not handling this meeting with professional style, but something about this man made her too emotional to care.

Anyway, once this useless interview was over, she wouldn't have to deal with him again.

"Well." She set the can of Coke down on the table. "I won't waste any more of your time. I just thought I'd let you know we're going to conduct a full-scale search for Spike. His picture is going to hit the papers tomorrow, and Kitty Krunchies is even going to spring for some television time.''

''What, no pictures on milk cartons?''

''Very funny, MacClaine. You can joke all you want, but I don't think the agency had anything to do with Spike's disappearance.''

''I'm not saying they did. It could have been some-one at Kitty Krunchies.'' He leaned forward, blue eyes intent, his hand going up to steady Jade against the sudden movement. ''All I'm saying is that Spike has done a damn good job selling that stuff, and he's never been late for dinner in the four and a half years I've had him. His contract comes up for renegotiation, and boom, he's gone. I'd just like you to keep an open mind about the possibility that this might not be an accident.''

''Okay.'' She'd say anything to get on with this in-terview and get it over with. She belonged back in her office, looking out over the Century City skyline, not sitting in a breakfast nook with three parrots, a mutt and Kevin MacClaine.

She knew the minute the word was out of her mouth that he didn't believe her. He sighed, then leaned back in his chair and stared at the ceiling.

''Okay.'' He said the word softly, with almost no emotion. There was a slight pause, then he glanced back at her. ''I'll call you if Spike turns up, and I'll be doing everything I can to help the search in my own area.''

Gillian looked down at the tabletop. He wasn't all that bad a guy. They were just from two different planets. Not the normal, two-different-types-of-planets differences that were usually between men and women. She and Kevin were simply *different*.

"I'm sorry. I can see—"

The blue eyes were too intense.

"I think I can see how you might feel that way. All of us want Spike back, if for different reasons. But I can—" She could feel her throat tightening up, and cleared it as quietly as she could. "I can see how much you love your animals, and I hope Spike comes home soon."

He believed her. She could see it in his eyes, in the slow, lazy grin that spread across his face.

"Okay."

There was a wealth more warmth in the word.

"NASTY BREAK, BIRDY. Good thing you caught me." Dr. John Downey smiled down at the old lady standing anxiously in front of him.

"I'm so glad you were still here. Even Louella had gone." Birdy didn't get along with Louella, the crusty receptionist. She knew the woman thought she imposed on the doctor, what with all the strays she brought in. And Dr. Downey was a good man. He knew she was on a fixed income and charged her almost nothing for the work he did on her strays.

"Is he okay now?" Michael asked.

"He'll need plenty of rest. Keep him quiet and away from any other animals. He should be as good as new if you just let him heal."

Birdy opened her purse and reached for her wallet but Dr. Downey touched her hand, stilling any movement.

"This one's on the house. I won't write it up on the books, and that way Louella won't complain."

"Thank you, Doctor. I appreciate it."

"I know you do. Not many people rescue as many animals as you do, Birdy. It's the least I can do."

He carried the cat, in a large cardboard box, out into the waiting room and set him down on one of the chairs.

"You look worried, Doctor. Are you sure he's all right?" Birdy was exquisitely sensitive to others' moods. It was just the way she was.

"He'll be fine." As he massaged his temples, he spoke softly. "I'm leaving on vacation tomorrow morning. Hilary and I are going to Bermuda."

Birdy looked up at him. She didn't like Hilary at all, but the doctor was infatuated with her. Birdy had met her once when she had pulled up in her Porsche. She'd had a quick impression of glossy black hair, cool blue eyes, a red, pouting mouth and delicate, princesslike features.

Not at all the sort of woman for the doctor. He loved his work. Hilary looked like the sort of woman who didn't like to get her hands dirty.

"I'm thinking of asking her to marry me."

Oh, no. Birdy kept her face expressionless. If there was one thing she'd learned in her life, it was that you had to let people make their own mistakes, no matter how painful the outcome. Absently, she reached down and touched Michael's hair. He was kneeling beside the box, looking in at the tabby cat.

"I don't think she's going to say yes."

Oh, good. "Well, I wish you a happy and safe vacation, Doctor, no matter what happens. You work too hard, and you certainly need the rest."

He sighed, then seemed to snap out of his thoughts. "I'll be back at the end of the month, Birdy. I've talked to Dr. Gordon, and she says she'll take care of any animals you might bring in. Don't mind Louella, just deal directly with Dr. Gordon."

"Thank you, Doctor."

BENJAMIN MERRILL SAT at his desk, idly twirling a pencil. And wondering what Gillian's reaction was going to be to his proposal.

She isn't going to like this. Not one bit.

He'd known she was exactly what the agency needed when she had come in for her interview six years ago. He'd seen himself again at that age, all energy and enthusiasm and drive. Ambitious. Assertive. Headed straight for success.

But there was a downside to all that success if your life wasn't balanced. He'd hit bottom at forty, but if his instincts were right—and they usually were—Gillian was going to hit that same point a few years earlier than he had.

He'd watched her carefully over dinner the other night. He'd invited her to his home in Bel Air, and his wife, Ashley, had cooked an excellent meal. All the signs were there. Gillian had been restless. Nervous. Slightly agitated. And after dinner she had excused herself from the table and spent quite a bit of time in the bathroom.

He knew she was starting to have stomach troubles. He also knew that, despite a healthy social life, she hadn't had a date in almost a year and half.

"People shouldn't play God," Ashley had chided him gently when he had told her his plan that same night as they were getting ready for bed.

"Why not?" he'd answered, pulling her into his arms. "You certainly saved my life the day you walked into it."

And she had. He'd been working too hard, drinking too much, burning the proverbial candle at both ends and in the middle. One look at Ashley across the crowded restaurant and he had known he had to talk to her, make her go out with him. She'd been dining with another man, but he had managed to get her phone number.

He'd called her the next day.

She'd had some misgivings.

He'd talked her into dinner that same night.

She'd refused—at first. She'd told him she was all of thirty-three.

He'd told her he was fifty-one.

They'd gone out to dinner and had a marvelous time.

He proposed to her exactly six weeks to the day he first saw her, and they were quietly married, now blissfully happy.

Not a course of action he would recommend to everyone, but it had certainly worked for him. Ashley completed his life, made him want to come home at night, gave him a reason for all the work he'd done, the life he'd built for himself.

The icing on the cake had been when she'd told him she was expecting a child. Ben Merrill was going to become a father for the first time at the ripe old age of fifty-three.

And he was loving every minute of it.

He hadn't thought of butting into Gillian's life until the evening of the Kitty Krunchies Kat Food party. It had been a huge affair, and the new designs for the boxes, bags and cans had been unveiled.

He'd glanced around the room and saw that Gillian was fascinated by Kevin MacClaine.

And the same Mr. MacClaine could hardly keep his eyes off her whenever she wasn't looking at him.

Ben had checked with Ashley, as he had come to respect her superior instincts in these matters. Her observations had coincided with his.

Now Spike, the infamous Kitty Krunchies cat, had provided a perfect excuse.

Maybe Gillian wouldn't see through the whole thing. It was kind of ridiculous. If she really thought about it, she would see it wasn't necessary.

But hell, she needed a vacation. So did MacClaine, taking care of all those animals, week after week.

Perhaps, if one of them wasn't too bullheaded, they'd realize they could vacation with each other for the rest of their lives.

It was shameless. But he had to do it.

His secretary buzzed the intercom and he leaned forward and pressed the button.

"Yes, Maddie?"

"Gillian Sommers is here to see you. Shall I send her in?"

He smiled.

It might work. Sometimes you just had to have a little faith.

"Send her right in."

Chapter Two

"No."

It was exactly the word Ben Merrill had been prepared to hear, so he was ready with his counterattack.

"Kitty Krunchies is the most important account we have."

"Absolutely not. Chase around the country with Kevin MacClaine looking for a lost cat? Ben, I've done a lot of things for you, but this is not going to be one of them."

"I'll take care of your other accounts while you're gone."

"Ben, come on. MacClaine can take care of this himself."

"I want you on this, Gillian. I need to know exactly how close we are to finding that cat. No Spike, no deal. No deal, and the bottom line is that the agency loses money. I still haven't told Charles that Spike is missing, and I don't want him to find out."

She was weakening, he could see it. Charles MacKay was one tough customer, the CEO of Kitty Krunchies. Ben could tell by the expression in Gillian's green eyes that she was considering the devastating consequences should Charles find out his famous fluffy spokesperson was gone.

Ben pushed the final button.

"I wouldn't want you to have to face Charles and tell him Spike is no longer available for filming."

That did it. A healthy dose of good old all-American fear.

"Oh, my God."

He almost felt sorry for her as she folded into her chair and leaned her head back against the high head-rest. Almost. Gillian was too tired. She could do worse than hit the road with MacClaine. He looked like a fun sort of guy.

"He'll be here any minute." As long as he was on a roll, he might as well get this entire thing set up.

She opened one eye, then closed it, defeated. "All right. I'll hit the road with Kevin, but there may be nothing left of both of us by the time this Spike hunt is through."

"He's that bad?"

"He's not that bad. It's just that he's . . . not really my type of person. We don't really see anything the same way. I've never liked those daredevil athletic types, you know, the guys in high school who would take on any challenge you gave them. I never credited them with having much upstairs."

Unfortunately her eyes were closed, and the gestures Ben made were completely ignored.

"Hello, Ben. I couldn't find your secretary, so I just walked in."

Gillian froze. Though she'd only talked to him twice, and briefly both times, she recognized the voice.

Kevin MacClaine.

She wondered how much he'd heard.

The thought of facing Charles MacKay paled in comparison to being stuck on the road with this man after having insulted him.

There was really nothing she could do but plow ahead.

She stood up, then glanced at his face. He'd heard her. There was something in those dark blue eyes bordering on dislike.

He's probably not much more thrilled at the prospect of being stuck with me. So we're even.

"All set, MacClaine?"

"Ready to go."

"So is Gillian."

"Ben!" Corbin said as he rushed into the office. "I have a theory as to what may have happened to Spike. My girlfriend was watching a special the other night, something about Satanism. She said the thought crossed her mind that Spike may have been a victim of a satanic cult. According to what Geraldo said—"

"Leave a memo on my desk."

Gillian had been covertly watching Kevin during this exchange, and she was surprised to see something akin to instant dislike toward Corbin. As long as she had known him, Corbin could be a real pain, but she was surprised by the instant antipathy Kevin seemed to feel toward him.

Corbin left the office, hot on the trail of this new idea. He loved writing memos, loved anything that basically attracted attention to himself. He was the sort of man who overshadowed any of the women in his life, having to be the center of attention.

"So," Ben said quietly, eyeing both of them. "I'll be available at home or at the office, twenty-four hours a day. You have my beeper number. Just find Spike as soon as possible."

"How do we know where to go?" Gillian wasn't asking out of any sort of defiance. She just wanted to know what she was getting into.

"I'll tell you where to go." This from Kevin, said so innocently that had she not seen the devilish glint in his eyes she might have thought it was a totally innocent remark.

Ben glanced from Kevin to Gillian, then cleared his throat to get their attention. "Kevin has a beeper and a number. We have three people taking care of the hotline. Its number is on hundreds of posters all over the city. Also, we're going with local television coverage."

"What about MacKay?" Gillian pressed. "How is all this going to keep him from finding out?"

Ben leaned forward, his palms flat on the surface of his desk. "He'll have to know, sooner or later. It's only a matter of days at this point. And we only have two weeks to get Spike back in time for filming. My sources tell me MacKay's vacationing with his wife and children in Bermuda. Then they're going to Disney World on the way back. He's very conscious of giving his family quality time. No one dares disturb him while he's on vacation, it's something of a company rule."

"If they find out Spike is missing, they might make an exception. But I'm counting on their desire to comply with MacKay's wishes winning out. Unless he has a satellite dish at the hotel, we have a little time until the news breaks."

Ben turned his attention to Kevin. "Will things be all right at the compound while you're on the road?"

"Everything's under control. Samantha is taking care of the animals."

"Hmm. Lovely woman. I remember her from the party."

"She's terrific."

Samantha. Gillian found herself searching her memory, trying to come up with a memory of the elusive Samantha. She remembered long, tawny-gold hair, a slender, strong figure, high cheekbones and slightly slanted, vivid green eyes.

Samantha had impressed her as the type of woman who could play six games of raquetball and barely pause for breath. She probably didn't even sweat.

Perfect. The jockette for the jock. Typical, they all like blond bimbos anyway.

She wondered why it even mattered to her who Kevin was involved with. They were from different worlds, and as soon as this cathunt was over, they would return to those worlds.

She understood why Ben wanted this entire problem solved as soon as possible. But she didn't quite fathom why he was so eager to push her out the door.

"Any other questions?" This from Ben.

"No," Kevin replied quietly.

"No," Gillian said.

"All right." Ben gave them both a long, measuring glance, then picked up a small sheaf of papers that had been lying on his desk. "The first place you'll be heading is Palm Springs. We've had some reports that Spike is at a house in Palm Desert and another call from Palm Springs. You can stay at my condo—"

"What?" Gillian could feel herself beginning to panic. She hated any disruption of the orderly life she'd built for herself. "I thought I got to go home every night! You mean this is like a real trip?"

"The way that I understand it," Kevin said slowly, "is that we simply drive to wherever the leads on Spike are. Right?"

Gillian could feel her entire world crumbling beneath her feet. Not only had she insulted the man she'd be cooped up with in a car for the next few weeks, but she wasn't even going to be able to use her home as a place she could crawl back to and recuperate.

Endless hours with Kevin flashed before her eyes. It would be different if he were her type, if there was just enough sexual chemistry to make this trip something of a feminine challenge. She knew she didn't get out enough, that her social life was in a shambles. But this wasn't the way to correct it, a road trip with Jungle Jim.

"So call me if you have any trouble. Gillian, you have a company credit card, Kevin has a beeper and the company car is right out—"

"We're taking my Jeep." Kevin stated this as a fact not to be argued with.

Ben was silent for a measuring instant, then said, "Do you have a car phone in case I need to reach you?"

"The beeper's good enough."

Gillian watched the two men square off, the way she watched men in the business world operate with each other every day. Ben was a formidable opponent, with years in the advertising business in his favor. Kevin was much younger and much less the businessman type.

Yet, to her complete and utter surprise, Ben backed down.

"Fine. Well, good luck to both of you."

HE DID OPEN THE JEEP'S DOOR for her. Gillian had to admit that, despite what she'd said about him, the guy had impeccable manners.

Maybe, just maybe, he hadn't heard what she'd said.

As she sat down in the passenger seat, she saw a small canvas bag on the seat behind her.

"That's all you're taking?" she asked as Kevin climbed into the driver's seat.

"What, now you're going to criticize the way I pack?"

He'd heard. She could feel a flush start to burn her cheeks and cursed her redhead's complexion. Her skin was so pale, every embarrassed emotion showed.

"I'm sorry. What I said in Ben's office was inexcusable."

"Hey, don't make it worse by apologizing. You think what you think."

"But there's no excuse for—"

"Look." Now all vestiges of that grin or the devilish light in his eyes were long gone. "We're stuck together until we find Spike. That doesn't mean we have to like each other. It simply means we have to get the job done. And the sooner the job gets done, the sooner you and I can say goodbye. So let's make the process as quick and painless as possible, okay?"

She felt as if all the breath had been squeezed out of her. Her stomach hurt. Suddenly, in the most childlike way, she wanted Kevin to like her. She wanted to like him.

This trip was going to be impossible.

But instead of voicing her thoughts, Gillian merely replied, her voice very small.

"Okay."

BEN WATCHED THE JEEP LEAVE the underground parking structure below the building. As the vehicle pulled into traffic, he stared at it and hoped that Gillian would forgive him should she learn of the deception.

The intercom buzzed, and he picked it up.

"Ashley's on the line."

"Thanks, Maddie."

"How did things go, Ben?"

"They're on their way to the condo in Palm Springs."

"Very nice. Even a romantic setting."

He laughed softly, remembering weekends they'd spent there. "How are you feeling?"

"Fine."

He glanced out the window again, trying to catch sight of the Jeep, but he couldn't see it anymore.

"I hope I did the right thing," he said. "I hope they don't manage to kill each other before they discover how much they fascinate each other."

"WHY ARE YOU taking all that?" Kevin asked as Gillian appeared in the living room of her town house, a large soft-sided bag in one hand and a tote in the other.

"Why don't we just agree to stop making comments about each other?" She didn't feel good; her stomach was acting up. And Kevin's comment didn't make her feel any better, though she supposed she deserved it and more after the crack she'd made about empty-headed jocks.

"We should just be gone over the weekend. Why two bags?"

He wasn't going to leave it alone. "It's really none of your business. Let's get going. The sooner we get to Palm Springs and find Spike, the sooner you don't have to worry about my packing."

"Fine." He got up off the couch in one fluid, graceful motion, then started toward her. She was surprised when he took the larger bag and started out the front door for the Jeep.

They were on the road and heading toward the 10 East when Gillian said, "I have to stop at a drugstore."

"For more stuff."

"Yes, for more stuff."

He was quiet after that. They turned into the local Sav-on Drugstore, and Gillian was surprised when he got out of the Jeep and began to lock his door.

"You don't have to go with me."

"Oh, I don't know. I might find some stuff myself that I have to take to the desert."

"You're very funny." But the twinkle in his eyes was reassuring. It seemed he wasn't that mad with what she'd said in Ben's office. But then why should he be? People didn't have to like each other in order to work together.

Inside, she headed straight for the upset stomach aisle. Once there, Gillian began filling the red plastic basket with Pepto Bismol, Maalox, Tums, Milk of Magnesia, and anything else she thought might do some good.

There was nothing as frightening as being away from her medicine cabinet.

"What the hell are you preparing for, a major attack?"

She glanced up to find Kevin watching her, a concerned expression on his face. One quick look at what he had in his basket convinced her that the sooner they were finished with this harebrained scheme, the better.

Barbecue potato chips. A six-pack of Coke. A large carton of malted milk balls, several other candy bars, a box of granola bars, a bottle of suntan lotion and a bottle of tanning oil.

"How can you put all that junk in your stomach?" she asked.

"I could ask you the same question. These are provisions for the trip."

She angled her chin up ever so slightly, hoping she looked a bit haughty and not ridiculous. "Well, these are my provisions."

"Do you have a stomach problem?"

"No, not really. It just pays to be . . . prepared."

"I see."

They paid for their purchases and were on the road a few minutes later.

"Granola bar?"

"No thanks."

Silence reigned for the next few miles. Gillian had to admit he was a good driver. For all his seeming like the swaggering, daredevil jock type, he was careful, if a little too fast. But she liked to drive fast, too, so who was she to judge?

"Want a Coke?"

"No, no thank you."

Silence.

What was she going to talk to this man about for the next few hours it took them to get to the desert? How could Ben have put her in this position?

"Some malt balls?"

"No." Her stomach was starting to hurt.

"You hungry?"

"No, not really."

"I am."

"After all that stuff?"

"That was just a snack. An appetizer. Did you eat breakfast?"

"You sound like someone's mother."

"Did you?"

"No,' Gillian admitted.

"And you're not hungry? No wonder you have stomach problems."

"I don't have stomach problems. I just believe in being prepared—"

"There's a McDonald's at the next exit."

"Yuck."

"I suppose you don't like Denny's, either."

"Not really. I'm not the hamburger type."

"And what type are you?"

She decided to really annoy him.

"Sushi."

"Raw fish?"

"Yep."

"Whatever gets you through the night."

"I take it you don't like it."

"I've eaten it."

"But you didn't like it."

"Not as much as a hamburger and fries, no."

"I knew it."

And at that exact moment, she knew she'd lit his fuse.

"Don't pigeonhole me, Gillie."

"Don't call me Gillie."

"Why not? Gillian sounds like an old lady. You look like a Gillie. Or you would look like a Gillie if you let your hair down and got out of one of those suits of yours."

"I knew it. Fine. Let's get it all out in the open now so that we really know what it is we think of each other and then leave it alone.

"I think you're a nice enough guy, but totally not my type. I didn't like the jocks when I was in high school, and I don't like them now. I've never in my life been attracted to men who use their muscles more than their brains. Is that enough for you? Oh, and by the way, this whole stupid idea was *not* mine, I didn't even want to go. I hope you find Spike, but I don't understand why I have to be trapped in a car with a man who finds me so endlessly, *insultingly* amusing."

Silence again.

"There. I said what I had to say. Now you go."

He took a deep breath, but even the pause before he spoke didn't prepare her for his next words.

"I think you're a stuck-up, judgmental prig. I think you've been working in advertising so long you don't know how to judge people except by the most purely superficial standards. You're the female equivalent of a stuffed shirt and I'd bet money you don't even know how to have a good time."

She took a breath, forgetting he'd allowed her to have her say, wanting more than anything to stop his tirade of words. Words that hit a little too close to home.

But he was quicker.

"I'll even go out on a limb, Gillie, and tell you that I was attracted to you at that damn Krunchies party. I thought you were one good-looking woman, and you got me going. But the minute we were introduced and you gave me that cool, holier-than-thou look, I lost interest. Completely. Because if there's one thing I can't stand in this life, it's a snob."

She was really hurting now, so she lashed back.

"You couldn't make it with a woman like me, even if you wanted to. I'm *glad* this is all out in the open. Now we don't even have to pretend to like each other. You can just find Spike and get back to your jockette girlfriend where you belong!"

"Jockette girlfriend?"

"Samantha." There was a wealth of emotion in the single word.

"A jockette? She'd be amused. What the hell do you have against staying in shape? She's a trainer, same as me. It's part of our work."

"Why didn't you ask her along instead of me?" Gillian knew this conversation was getting totally out of control. Gillian Sommers, one of the best advertising minds at the Merrill Agency, was arguing with a jock in his Jeep like a five year old.

"Someone had to keep the home fires burning. Besides, I trust her to take care of things. Who's looking after the town house while you're gone?"

She considered making up a fictitious boyfriend, and plunged ahead.

"Henry's taking care of things while I'm gone."

Kevin didn't have to know that Henry was her goldfish, given to her as a present at the annual office Christmas party. He was being taken care of by Maddie, Ben's secretary, while she was on this trip.

"Henry, eh? What's he like?"

She thought quickly. *The fattest goldfish in the Western Hemisphere.*

"He's—elegant." She thought of the chubby little goldfish swimming quickly through the water. "Very smooth moves. He impressed me right from the start."

"Where did you meet him?"

"At the office Christmas party."

"What does he do?"

"He—he made a lot of money...swimming. Now he doesn't have to work at all. Other people take care of him."

"So you go for those rich types. I guess I had you pigeonholed, too."

"I guess you did. We're even."

"One more thing."

"Be my guest."

"I hate the way you dress. Why don't you dress like a woman, instead of in those suits?"

"I'll have you know this is an Armani."

"I don't care what it is. Don't you have any casual clothes?"

Gillian sat up a little straighter and looked out the windshield. She was going to kill Ben when she returned to the office.

"I'm still representing the Merrill Agency, no matter where we are."

"We're looking for a *cat*, Gillie. When you deal with animals, you tend to get a little bit dirty. You aren't in your office now."

"What a mind. So quick."

She could feel his gaze on her, and she willed herself to keep looking out the windshield, concentrating on the road in front of them.

"We've both had our say," he said quietly. "The least we can do for each other is to be polite and consider the fact that *neither* of us wants to be in this position."

"Fine."

"Okay."

"All right."

Silence.

Almost twenty minutes later Kevin announced, "I take it you're still not hungry, so I'm pulling off at the next exit and getting myself a sub."

"Fine." Gillian softened her voice while she said the one word, not really wanting to fight with him anymore.

They were in Riverside now, and the area Kevin drove through after he exited off the freeway looked like a quiet patch of suburbia, a small college town. A number of fast-food places lined the street, and Kevin pulled into one called Delia's Subs.

"You want anything?"

It was a beginning. They had to work together. And so far, Kevin was being more of a gentleman than she had been a lady. Gillian really didn't want to argue with him anymore. She made up her mind quickly.

"Sure. I'll come in and get something to drink."

The sub shop was immaculate, done up in red and with masses of hanging plants. Kevin walked straight up to the counter, and Gillian overheard him order a large roast beef sub, a large Coke, and an order of fries.

She was still standing, studying the menu, when he walked up beside her.

"They make their own bread."

"Mmm."

"It's not sushi, but it's the best sub place in Riverside."

She continued to study the menu.

"The first place we have to stop is just outside Palm Desert, so it might be a little while before we can get something to eat."

That did it. "I'll eat something."

She ordered turkey on whole wheat, hold the mayo and oil and heavy on lettuce, tomatoes and sprouts.

Gillian took extra napkins before she headed to the booth Kevin was sitting in. He was sipping his Coke and looking out the window. A whole flock of people in their early twenties sped by on bikes. The treelined street looked like something out of the fifties.

"It must be a college town," she remarked as she sat down.

"The university's just down the street."

They were silent as Gillian carefully spread out napkins over the skirt of her suit. She loved beautiful clothes, and this suit was no exception. A silvery gray, the suit was made of a wool crepe about as heavy as an egg white. The short, single-breasted jacket and slim skirt were perfect for the office, as was the delicate silk blouse.

But now, remembering Kevin's words back in the Jeep, Gillian wondered if she should have packed as many suits as she had. She'd thought this trip was going to amount to purely business, and she knew the Merrill Agency had a reputation to uphold. She'd thought they were going on a typical Merrill business trip.

But this trip was turning out to be anything but typical. Maybe, just maybe, she should have packed a pair of slacks.

She didn't dare tell Kevin she didn't own a pair of jeans.

"I'll get our order," he said suddenly, then got up and walked toward the counter.

She turned and looked out the window. A young, college-age man and woman were walking slowly down the street, holding hands and licking ice-cream cones. There wasn't anything especially remarkable about them, except for the fact that they only had eyes for each other. They were so engrossed with each other nothing else seemed to matter.

And to her surprise, Gillian felt her throat start to tighten up. There was something so innocent about young love. She supposed everyone thought that way once, until they realized the world could be a very dangerous place and all love stories didn't necessarily have happy endings. . . .

"Are you on one of those diets or something?" This from Kevin. She turned her head, blinked her eyes a few times to clear away the slight moisture that had gathered, then shook her head.

"I just like eating healthy food."

"Then we're in trouble again."

He was actually grinning. She couldn't believe it. What did this man find so amusing about their entire situation?

"Let me in on the joke." She stuck a straw into the plastic top of her Sprite and took a sip. She couldn't see how Kevin drank all that Coke, there was so much caffeine in it.

"It's funny, Gillie. When you really look at the entire situation—I mean, except for poor Spike—the whole thing is pretty funny."

"I guess it is."

Kevin swallowed another bite of his sandwich. "Look at it this way. In a million years, neither of us would have gone out with the other. We're totally different, we don't turn each other on—"

"You liked me at the party. I turned you on until you met me." She couldn't resist reminding him. As petty as it seemed, she realized she didn't want him to forget he had once been attracted to her.

"Well, yeah. Sure. But aside from that one moment of insanity, we never would have met, let alone spent this much time together."

"True."

"And now here we are. All because of Kitty Krunchies. I have to admit, it's one of the things I like about life, its total unpredictability. It keeps things from getting dull."

"I can't *stand* not knowing what I'm going to be doing— Why are you laughing?"

He picked up a French fry and popped it in his mouth. "This is going to be a challenge to both of us, seeing how long we can get along. It's like a crew in a submarine. Tensions mount, tempers flare—"

"You're crazy—"

"People start to do bizarre things—"

"We're not in a submarine—"

"Think about it Gillie. This is probably the one time in both our lives when we have an up-close look at how

the other half lives. How other people think and feel
and operate. This is going to be a great experience.''

She smiled slightly. ''You don't think like anyone
I've ever met.''

He smiled back, that same satisfied grin, like the cat
that ate the canary. And she found herself starting to
melt. Just a little.

He was kind of cute, in a bizarre kind of way. Not
her type at all, but she could see how Samantha could
have been attracted to him.

''What do you and Samantha do when you're together?'' she asked him suddenly.

''Sam and I?'' He started to laugh then, and when
he was back under control, he said, ''A little of this, a
little of that. We talk about animal training a lot, so
much so that we drive other people crazy. I don't
know, we do what most people do when they're together. Sometimes we take Johanna to the zoo, show
her the animals.''

''Who's Johanna?''

''Her daughter.''

''You have a child.''

''No. But if I ever have one I'd want her to be like
Johanna. She's something. Five years old and she's
going to take the art world by storm. One time when I
was watching her, we painted an entire wall off my
hallway. With crayons, of course.''

''You *are* crazy.''

''That's what Sam said. But she laughed when she
saw the wall.''

"Do you love her?" Gillian was surprised at herself for asking such a personal question, but she had to know.

"Yeah, I do. Sam and I go way back."

"How long have you known her?"

"Almost seven years."

Gillian thought quickly. "So she had a child with another man while she was with you?"

"No, it wasn't quite like that."

She thought she was prying, so she concentrated on her food and finished off her sandwich. She was just swallowing the last bite when Kevin said, "So, this Henry guy. The rich swimmer. Are you going to marry him?"

"He hasn't asked me."

"Do you think he's going to?"

"We've been together almost three years."

"What kind of stuff do you two do together?"

"We hang out around my house a lot. Watch TV. I fix him meals. The usual."

Once they were finished, Kevin bought a few freshly baked chocolate-chip cookies for the road and they resumed their journey.

Within another hour, they were outside Palm Desert.

"This woman lives just outside town, a few exits before Ben's condo. She says this tabby cat came to her door and they've been feeding it. Just think, if it really is Spike we can just pick him up and drive back home. We'll never have to argue again."

"Yeah." But as Gillian looked out the window at the small houses they were passing, she wondered if that was what she really wanted.

Chapter Three

The cat in question was not Spike.

"Y'know, I *thought* she looked a little young," the woman in curlers said. She was painfully thin and dressed in tight jeans and a stained, stretched-out pink T-shirt. Three children under the age of five were camped around the television set in the other room, sprawled all over the large couch.

"Are you going to keep her?" Kevin asked. The woman had made them some coffee, and they were sitting in the small, clean kitchen. The room smelled faintly of bleach and baby powder, but the back door was ajar and a hot, desert breeze was blowing in.

The tabby kitten was sitting on Kevin's blue-jeaned thigh, and he was stroking her spine and making her purr, a soft, rumbling sound.

The woman's faded blue eyes clouded slightly. "No, I can't. Joe says we have enough trouble feeding the kids. He was mad when I took that little baby in and bought her some food."

"I'm thankful you did. It could have been Spike."

"It weren't nothing."

"Please let me reimburse you," Kevin said quietly, and Gillian watched as he wrote out a check and handed it to the woman after she told him the amount of money she'd spent on food and litter.

"So, you own Spike?" she said after it had been decided Kevin would take the kitten with them.

"Yes, Spike's my cat. I found him in an animal shelter. It was his last day there. The minute I saw him, I knew I couldn't let him die."

"I know that feeling," the woman responded eagerly. "When this little one came to the door, I couldn't just leave her." A soft blush stained her cheeks. "I knew she wasn't your Spike. But," she said, rushing on hopefully, "I thought maybe if y'all couldn't find him, you could use this one as soon as she grows a little."

"I appreciate the thought."

"I just love those commercials, especially the ones where he's so fussy about his food."

"Thank you."

"Did you buy Kitty Krunchies?" Gillian asked, then took a sip of the coffee the woman had offered them. She usually didn't touch caffeine, but it seemed rude to refuse this woman's hospitality.

"Oh, no! Not for a baby! I got her that soft food in those little pop-top cans. I thought it would be better for her."

"She looks fine to me," Kevin said. "You did a good job."

The woman smiled, then said, "I have to ask, what with you folks living near Hollywood and all. Do y'all know Burt Reynolds?"

GILLIAN WAS SURPRISED by the amount of time they spent there. She'd thought once it was decided the kitten was not Spike, she and Kevin would have headed straight for Ben's condominium. But as she sipped her coffee, she had to admire the way Kevin talked with the woman.

When they left, it was only about an hour until sunset.

"Looks like a storm coming," the woman said. "Y'all be careful on the road."

"We will be. And you give me a call if you change your mind and decide you want a kitten."

Kevin carried the kitten on his shoulder until they reached the Jeep, then he put the little animal in a cat carrier and set it on the back seat.

"I'm going to rearrange our luggage so that this one has a little more room."

"Fine." Gillian watched him as he rearranged their bags, then strapped the cat carrier to the seat with a seat belt. Something about the way he'd talked to that lonely woman had touched her. She was used to living her life at a breakneck pace, rushing from one project to the next. There was so much in life she just hadn't made time for.

Yet she was sure that Kevin, having sensed this woman was starved for adult company, took all the time in the world for what he considered to be important.

"C'mon, get in and we'll beat the storm."

"Isn't there a cover for this thing?"

"I'll put it up if it starts to rain."

They pulled back onto the freeway, but as they neared their exit, big fat drops of rain began to fall.

"It's not supposed to rain in the desert," she said.

"Tell that to the clouds. We're not that far from the exit. Once we're off the freeway, I'll pull over and get the top up."

Once they exited, Kevin was as good as his word. There was some road construction going on, and they went over a few hard bumps, but once they were out of direct traffic and could pull over, Kevin did and put up the top.

"Did you get too wet?" he called to her from the back of the Jeep.

"Not very. Do you need help?"

"No. I'll be done in a minute."

This actually wasn't too bad. She could get along with Kevin. So maybe he wasn't her type, he still had his good points. All people didn't have to be alike. She could get along with all kinds of people if she put her mind to it—

"Gillie, we lost your bag."

"What?"

Kevin had climbed in and was sitting in the driver's seat. He was soaked, his dark blond hair plastered to his head, his wet jeans and navy T-shirt molded to his body.

"Which bag?"

"The big one."

"My clothes!"

"We'll go back for it. We'll find it, I promise."

They drove in tense silence for a while, until Gillian saw the dark lump in the other lane.

"There it is! Pull over!"

She was already starting to get out of the car and run onto the highway when she felt Kevin's arms come around her tightly.

"No, Gillie—"

She hadn't even seen the truck that was now coming straight toward her suitcase.

"No!"

The first big wheel of the rig connected with her bag and Gillian watched in horror as the seams split. Then the second wheel finished the job, dragging the bag for a short distance before the truck lumbered on.

"Ahhhh!"

She struggled aginst his hold, not totally believing what she'd seen. Kevin released her, and they both ran across the four-lane highway in the pouring rain toward the flattened bag.

Gillian reached it first and dragged it to the shoulder of the road. It was a pitiful sight. The bag was totally destroyed, her shampoo and conditioner had exploded throughout the clothing, along with a large bottle of body lotion and a small bottle of bubble bath. Oil and dirt from the tires had been pressed into most of the delicate wool jackets, skirts and blouses. She dug through the bag frantically, and managed to pull a mangled pump loose, then sat down in the wet, sandy earth next to her suitcase and started to cry.

She felt Kevin's arm go comfortably around her shoulder and something inside her snapped.

"You!" She turned all her frustration and anger on him.

"Gillie, come on. I admit I hate the way you dress, but this would be a drastic measure even for me—"

"You did this deliberately! You made sure my bag would fall off the Jeep so all the clothes you hate would be destroyed! Are you happy now?"

"Gillie, you're tired—"

"Are you happy, now that wherever we go I'm going to look like one of the Beverly Hillbillies—"

"Gillie, you're getting soaked. Come on, let's go to the Jeep—"

Gillian grabbed what was left of her suitcase and struggled on ahead of him.

"Let me get that—"

"Why, so you can throw it back in the road? Maybe another truck will come along!"

"Come on, Gillie, you're not being fair—"

"*This* isn't fair! *Me* being on the road with *you* isn't fair! I don't *belong* on a chase like this, I want to go *back* to my office where it's *safe* and *warm* and I *never* have to see *you*—"

Her heel caught in some soft earth and she stumbled. Completely furious, she took off her leather pump and flung it into the bushes on the side of the road.

"I hate this!"

He came up behind her so swiftly she didn't have a chance. One minute she was stumbling along the shoulder of the road, one pump on, one pump off, dragging her mangled suitcase. The next, Kevin scooped her up over his shoulder and picked up her suitcase with his other hand. Then he began to walk down the road with a purposeful stride.

By the time they reached the Jeep, she'd calmed down a little.

Kevin flung what was left of Gillian's suitcase into the back seat, then set her down in front of him, holding her tightly against him.

"Gillie, look at me."

She did, then reached up and pushed her hair out of her eyes.

"I may have made some remarks about the way you dress, but I would have never willfully destroyed your clothing."

She nodded her head slowly, realizing as the adrenaline began to ebb that she'd behaved pretty badly. They were both soaked, but it was a warm, moist rain, so they weren't shivering with cold.

His eyelashes were spiky, his clear blue eyes direct and intense. Kevin was looking at her as if suddenly he was seeing her again for the first time. She watched as his gaze dropped to her mouth, then back to her eyes, then to her mouth....

He wanted to kiss her.

He looked into her eyes for a moment, then something shifted, changed. He stepped back, releasing his hold on her.

"I'm sorry it happened," he said. "But I couldn't let you run out in front of that truck for a bag of clothes."

"I didn't see the truck," she said, then her legs started to shake as she realized what would have happened if Kevin hadn't thought fast and grabbed her.

His arms came around her again, only this time he pulled her gently against him. Gillian took a deep breath as her arms went up around his neck and she relaxed against him. She closed her eyes, her cheek against the wet cotton of his T-shirt. His skin felt warm, even through his soaked clothing.

His hands were steady, his touch gentle. Gillian rubbed her cheek against his shirtfront and marveled at the way they fit together. He was tall enough so that she could rest her head on his chest while they were standing against each other. His chin came right to the top of her head.

She'd shot up in the eighth grade to her full height of five seven, and it had seemed that, until this moment, none of the men she'd been with had been the right height. Or fit.

She shivered again, this time more from cold than fear.

"Come on. Let's get in the Jeep. I've got a blanket in the back you can wrap up in, then we can get to Ben's and get you in a hot bath."

GILLIAN LEFT HER ORPHAN PUMP in the Jeep, and when she stumbled on a sharp stone and cried out, Kevin carried her up the stairs and, after pausing to unlock the door, directly into the bathroom.

He turned on the light and the heater, then left her to retrieve the kitten and their luggage.

The bathroom was all silver and white, high tech and functional. The first thing Gillian did was walk over to the large mirror over the double sink and look at herself.

How could Kevin have wanted to kiss her? Her copper-colored hair, usually restrained in a business-like, dress-for-success style, was tumbling around her shoulders in a riot of waves. There were dark smudges under her green eyes. The rain had washed off all traces of the carefully applied makeup she usually wore.

But she looked wonderful.

There was something so alive in her eyes, something that hadn't been there before. A certain tenseness had left her expression, and she wondered at the fact that she was usually so controlled.

Except around him.

She didn't usually behave like a complete witch with men. Usually she was quietly controlled, listening, always aware of capturing and maintaining the upper hand. She usually revealed as little about herself as possible, not wanting the relationship to deepen before she had a chance to decide if she wanted it to or not.

This was so different from anything she'd ever experienced.

The knock on the door took her out of her thoughts.

"Are you decent?"

"Yes."

He came into the bathroom carrying her suitcase. Then he set it down on the floor and worked the zipper open as far as he could. When the bag still wouldn't open, he pulled up a leg of his jeans and reached for the knife he had strapped to his cowboy boot.

Gillian watched in silence as he ripped open what was left of her suitcase. He wielded the knife with an expert's touch, and she wondered at this man and his unusual talents.

Not many of the advertising types she knew would have reacted so quickly and saved her from running out in front of a truck. They could work out in their incredibly sophisticated gyms as long as they liked, but the only way a man honed instincts like Kevin's to such a fine edge was by working with them every day.

"There. I don't think there's much you'll be able to salvage, but if you let me know what you need, I'll run over to the mall and pick up some clothes for you."

The thought of this man picking out clothes for her was embarrassing.

"No, that's all right. I'll just take a quick shower and—"

"And what? Put on those wet clothes? Gillie, you don't even have a pair of shoes."

When she didn't answer, he said quietly, "I'm not embarrassed about it if you aren't. I have three sisters."

She had to smile. One of her first impressions had been correct. He was a man who got straight to the point.

"I'm not even embarrassed buying tampons."

"All right. Let me see what I can salvage."

She'd known that there wouldn't be much. As she pulled each piece of ruined clothing out of the canvas duffel bag, she handed it to Kevin. He'd searched the kitchen until he'd found a large, plastic garbage bag, and the ruined clothing went directly into the bag.

When she got to her underwear, she was only mildly embarrassed. She could try and salvage some of it, if she soaked it right away and then washed it out by hand.

"Why did you pack so much underwear?" he asked suddenly.

This entire day had been so crazy and she was so tired that there was no further energy for her to give over to embarrassment.

"It's kind of a security thing with me. I can face anything, knowing I have clean underwear."

They made a list.

"What size?"

"Ten."

"Shoes?"

"Seven and a half."

"Bra size?"

"Thirty-four B."

"Anything else before I go?"

"Covered rubber bands and bobby pins."

"I kind of like your hair down. Maybe I'll forget."

She gave him a look and he laughed.

"I'll pick up a pizza on the way home. Take care of Junior here until I get back."

She hadn't even noticed the tabby kitten sitting up on the toilet tank, watching the proceedings curiously.

"And I'll leave you a granola bar in case you get hungry."

He was almost out the door when she called his name.

"Kevin?"

"Yeah."

"Thanks."

THERE WAS JUST ENOUGH bubble bath in the squashed bottle so she was able to pour the contents under a steady stream of bath water. The scent of her favorite french perfume, composed completely of white flowers, filled the large bathroom.

Junior watched with great interest from the top of the toilet tank.

As Gillian eased her cold body into the warm, bubbly water, the sensation was so pleasurable she groaned. She still felt as if her body was vibrating gently, being bounced around in Kevin's Jeep. It felt good to be quiet, alone and sitting in a hot bath.

Closing her eyes, she ducked her head beneath the water and ran her fingers through her hair. It was a mass of snarls. Maybe Ashley had left some conditioner in one of the bathroom cabinets.

But for now, she didn't want to do much but lie in this cloud of scented bubbles and ease away all the aches in her body.

When she opened her eyes, she started, then laughed as she realized Junior was sitting on the edge of the tub. Seeing him out of the corner of her eye, he'd startled her.

"So, what do you think of yourself? Pretty smart, getting adopted by that lady and now Kevin. I bet you'll like it at the compound if you can manage to stay away from all his dogs."

The kitten blinked, then leaned over and batted a pile of bubbles with a tiny tabby paw.

"You'd better watch it or you'll fall in." She really was a pretty little cat. Her eyes were green-gold, full of life and curiosity, and the tiger markings were striking, dark gray stripes on a softer gray background. Her eyes were rimmed in black, and her nose was pink.

Junior merely batted at the bubbles again.

"If you fall in, it's your own fault." Gillie leaned back and closed her eyes. This was heaven. She rarely had time for bubble baths. Usually her morning began with a quick shower before she threw on her clothes and headed for work. Sometimes, if she felt really anxious at night, she'd take another shower, letting the hot spray of water massage the tense muscles in her shoulders and neck.

This kind of leisurely bath was a pleasurable enjoyment she rarely gave herself. Nothing to do, no phone calls to make, no strategy to plot, no reports to read. Nothing to do but lie in the hot water and soak away the last vestiges of the chilly rain.

She opened her eyes as Junior walked onto her shoulder and started to chew on her hair.

"Hey! Don't do that." She lifted the little cat, still purring, off her shoulder and placed her on the bathroom floor. Junior gave her a puzzled look.

"Are you hungry?"

The kitten opened its pink little mouth, and the tiniest of mews came out of it.

"Fine. Just let me soak for another minute—"

The kitten mewed again.

"Great."

She got out of the tub, careful that her wet feet hit the bathmat. Kevin had brought the rest of their luggage into the other room, and she remembered the woman giving him two cans of cat food she still had.

Gillian darted quickly into the living room, saw the brown paper bag and reached inside for one of the cans of cat food. Silently blessing the pop top—and wondering why the Kitty Krunchies Kanned Kat Food didn't use a similar type of opener—she popped the can open, walked back into the bathroom and threw the lid into the wastebasket, then set the opened can on the floor.

Junior darted over to the can as if magnetized to it and began to eat.

Her problems solved for the moment, Gillian added some more hot water to her bath and climbed back in. As she sank back she thought about Kevin.

He'd wanted to kiss her, she was sure of that. She'd seen it in his eyes, in the way he'd looked at her mouth. For just that instant in the rain, he'd wanted to kiss her.

Then why didn't he? She thought she already knew the answer to that one. Kevin wasn't the dummy she'd thought he was. He didn't want to mix business with pleasure. Suppose they were to get involved, a little fling while they searched for the missing Spike. Though little flings weren't really her style, maybe he'd thought about it. Maybe flings were his style. Maybe he and this Samantha had an open relationship.

As soon as she thought the words, she rejected them. One thing she'd seen in the short time she'd been with Kevin was that he genuinely liked women. Growing up in a home with three sisters, he would have had plenty of time to view them as individuals with intelligence and feelings.

He probably doesn't want to hurt Samantha.

She's lucky.

Gillian was surprised by the second thought. Kevin MacClaine was so much more than she'd given him credit for. He was a sensitive man, the way he'd spent time with the lonely woman today. He was strong and—well, *brave*. It wasn't every man who prevented a woman from running under a truck after a few Armani suits.

And he was smart. Maybe not in the way she thought smart was supposed to be, but maybe he was smart in a better sense. Kevin was smart about life, and no amount of education, no MBA could teach you that.

She got up again, being careful not to get the floor too wet, and searched through one of the cabinets until she found a protein pack for her hair. At least it would take out the tangles.

Getting back in the tub, Gillian opened up the packet, spread the stuff into her hair, piled it up on top of her head and lay back in the rapidly cooling water. She operated the spigots with her toes and turned on the hot water, heating up the bath just a little bit more.

Junior was finished with her meal and was making a determined effort to clean herself. Gillian watched the little cat for a while, her mind drifting, then pulled the plug and lay back in the bathtub as the water slowly drained out.

She finished with a stinging shower, rinsing all of the protein pack out of her hair. Then, one towel around her body and another turban-style around her hair, she padded into the other room to wait for Kevin.

HE'D HEARD ALL THE STORIES about men being embarrassed to buy women's underwear, and he still didn't understand them.

Once in the lingerie department in Bullocks, he'd given the saleslady one of Gillian's bras that wasn't too damaged, explained the situation, told her Gillian's sizes and sat down to wait while the woman gathered up some underwear.

What bothered him was that he'd wanted to kiss Gillian.

What bothered him even more was that she still turned him on but he wasn't so sure he liked her. And that wasn't fair to any woman.

When the saleslady returned, she showed him what she'd picked out.

"I'm sure it will all be fine."

"You can return anything that doesn't fit properly. Just keep the receipt."

He nodded his head. "Do you have anything— anything really beautiful. Something kind of elegant. I want to get her something to make up for losing all her clothes."

"What kind of clothing does she like?"

He thought for a second. "She wears Armani suits."

The saleslady's eyes widened appreciatively. "That's a very powerful look in Los Angeles. Very elegant. She might like something soft and elegant for just lounging around at home."

"Whatever you think. I'm open to suggestion."

The minute he saw it, he knew it was Gillie. The full-length, kimono-style robe was a deep emerald silk, the sash full and richly embroidered.

"I'll take it. Do you gift wrap?"

"Certainly."

He thought about what Gillian was going to say when she got a look at the other clothes he'd bought her. Not one jacket, not one skirt among them. Two pairs of jeans, a pair of Reeboks, some socks, a pair of thongs, two pairs of shorts, a sweatshirt, three tank tops, a one-piece bathing suit and a loud T-shirt that proclaimed, in black letters on a white background, Come on Vacation, Leave on Probation.

Not exactly her style, but these clothes made more sense for the type of trip they were on.

He thanked the saleslady as she handed him the bag, then headed toward the exit. Kevin started to grin as he pictured what Lynne would think about his buying underwear for a woman he wasn't even sure he liked.

He'd grown up in the Palm Springs area, gone to high school here. Lynne and Gil had been like a second set of parents to him, and he was friends with their three children.

But Lynne—she could still read him like a book. She was almost as good as his own mother at deciphering what was really going on. She still made the meanest pizza in Rancho Mirage—and was an incurable romantic.

It was a deadly combination.

"That pizza smells heavenly." Gillian had changed into a pair of jeans and the peach sweatshirt she'd found among all the clothes Kevin had bought for her. She couldn't fault his choices. Everything she'd tried on so far fit perfectly.

"Shakey's special. Salami, pepperoni, sausage, beef, mushroom and olive. Harpo would probably die for a piece."

"He really eats pizza?"

"He really does. He's such a pig, it's a wonder he doesn't burn himself with the cheese."

Gillian was familiar with the layout of Ben and Ashley's kitchen, so she quickly set the table and laid out glasses. Kevin had even bought a bottle of red wine, so he opened it and poured them both a glass.

"Here's to finding Spike, safe and sound," Gillian said, raising her wineglass in a toast.

"I'm with you."

"This is great pizza," she said later, after her third slice. "I haven't had pizza this good in a long time."

"With all the sushi you eat, I'm surprised you have it at all."

She glanced up at him. He was smiling at her. Teasing.

"You must have gotten in a lot of practice teasing your sisters."

"I tormented them all. It's a brother's job."

"Are you older, younger, what?"

"The second of four, surrounded by women. They're great. Kate's the oldest, she's a classical musician and lives in Boston with her husband and four children. I'm out here with the animals. Sharon got married and lives up around Santa Cruz. She's really into gardening, sewing, canning, all that stuff.

They have three kids, and she tells them the greatest stories. Mitch keeps trying to get her to write them down and get them published. And Kelly's the baby. She's a real rebel. She's living in New York right now. She wants to be a rock-and-roll star.''

He grinned as he reached for another slice of pizza. ''The last postcard I got from her said she might have a gig out here and she was planning on coming and crashing with me.''

''I bet it was fun, growing up the way you did.'' She couldn't imagine Kevin doing much of anything that wouldn't be fun.

''I heard it all. Men always talk about women's mystery. And they're right. I grew up with three women who let me in on everything, and I still can't figure the whole thing out.''

''What do your parents do?''

''Dad had his own business, an office supply store. Mom was his partner. All of us worked there summers and after school. He sold it when he retired, and now they're traveling. What about you?''

''I have two older brothers and one younger. My father was in advertising, my mother took care of everything at home.''

''Where are they now?''

''I think Bob's in Tucson, Jamie's married and lives in San Francisco, and John never really lets anyone know where he is.''

''Your parents?''

''My mother died when I was fifteen. My father died a few years ago.''

"That must have been hard on you. Were you kind of the substitute mother?"

"No, we had housekeepers." It was funny, she had the most overwhelming compulsion to tell Kevin how empty the big house in San Francisco had been. How lonely it had been in boarding school. How the holidays had never quite seemed like holidays. She imagined what his life growing up must have been like, and she couldn't help contrasting it with her own.

He'd never understand what it had been like. Kevin came from a background of warmth, laughter and love. People who had it all while they were growing up couldn't understand how empty it was when you didn't.

She'd never hated her father; he'd just been unable to cope with the highly emotional teenager she'd been. If she were totally honest with herself, her mother hadn't been much more equipped to raise children. They had been a cool, self-contained couple, and Gillian had often thought they had seen raising a family as something they were supposed to do, not something they could enjoy.

She'd stopped wondering about it long ago.

Kevin was looking at her in a way that was making her decidedly uncomfortable. As if he saw too much. She decided to change the subject.

"Do you think she'll make it?" At his puzzled look, she explained herself. "Kelly."

"You know, the frightening thing is, I really think she will. She was singing before she could talk, and once music videos hit, you couldn't pry her away from the television with a crowbar. She begged Dad to take her to some of the rock concerts, because he wouldn't let her go alone when she was younger. He didn't have the stamina for that kind of music, so I was drafted into service.''

"You're a good guy."

"Ah, she loved it. She'd talk about the whole thing for days, she always had the radio going in her room. My folks got her a guitar for her thirteenth birthday and she taught herself to play with one of those books. Later on, she took lessons. I think she's going to do it.''

"You must be proud of her."

"Kelly? Yeah, she's great. She never complained when I brought home another animal that had to be fixed up. Kate and Sharon got a little frustrated with me, but Kelly was always helping me fix 'em up."

They finished the pizza, cleaned up the kitchen, then Gillian said, "I guess I should go try on the rest of my clothes and make sure they fit."

"Nah, don't do that. Let's go check out the pool."

She hesitated for just a second. "But we just ate. Is that a good idea?"

"So we'll dip our feet in the Jacuzzi first. If we wait a little bit, it won't be a problem."

"I don't have a suit."

"Check again. There's one on your bed." Kevin picked up his own small bag and headed for the other bedroom at the opposite end of the condominium. "I'll meet you in the living room in five minutes."

Even after his bedroom door closed, Gillian stood still in the living room. She hesitated.

Maybe he just wants some company. She wasn't really all that tired, not after the pizza. And after all, Kevin had run all over Palm Desert buying her clothes while she'd just been soaking in the tub.

Her mind made up, she headed back into her bedroom and searched through her bags until she found the suit. It was a simply cut one-piece in a vivid tropical print exploding with flamingos and palm trees. There was a large brilliantly colored parrot on the front, and she thought of Harpo.

It was like nothing she would have ever picked out for herself.

She tried it on. Like the other clothing, it fit perfectly. Gillian slipped on her thongs, then went to the mirror with the rubber bands and hair pins. It was no use getting her hair wet again.

She was just starting to braid her hair up when she caught sight of her reflection in the mirror.

"I kind of like your hair down."

Her fingers stilled as she studied her face in the mirror. So what if she got her hair wet? It would dry. Somehow, with the mass of coppery waves falling just below her shoulders, she did look . . .

Certainly sexier. Less prim.

Less like a stuffed shirt.

That one had hurt because she knew it was true. She knew she hid herself behind perfectly designed suits and silk blouses, hid the vibrant clouds of hair in severe, scraped-back styles.

She eyed herself critically in the mirror. The suit was so flamboyant; the thin, stretchy material hugged her body tightly. And as bodies went, hers wasn't bad. Her schedule was so frenetic, she didn't have a chance to put on an extra ounce of weight.

She hadn't been swimming in a long time. It usually didn't fit into her schedule.

"Hey, slowpoke. I said five minutes." Kevin's voice was teasing as it floated in from the living room.

Her mind made up, Gillian pulled her fingers through her hair, destroyed the beginning of the braid. She ran her brush through her hair, then watched as the waves settled around her shoulders.

"I'm coming."

Chickening out at the last minute, she grabbed Ashley's white terry-cloth robe off the hook in the bathroom. She threw it on, tightened the belt, then strode determinedly out to face Kevin.

Chapter Four

The desert night was cool, but the pool was heated. Gillian floated on her back and looked up at the stars. They were so bright in the sky. She couldn't see the stars this way in Los Angeles. She'd forgotten how beautiful they were.

Even swimming, she and Kevin were different. She walked down the pool steps slowly, immersing her body in stages. He went straight for the diving board and dove in, slicing through the water cleanly.

Now he was floating alongside her, both of them studying the sky.

"Why do you think Spike might be this far away from the compound?" she asked.

"I had a cat once that fell asleep in a moving van and ended up in Berkeley. Animals can do some pretty amazing things."

"Do you still think Spike was kidnapped?"

"I'm not sure. I'm just keeping the idea open as a definite possibility. *If* someone wanted Spike out of the picture, they'd make sure to dump him as far away from the compound as possible. That way he wouldn't be able to wander back."

"What about all those stories about animals traveling thousands of miles to get back to their owners?"

"They're true. But the more miles, the more dangers. Life isn't a Disney movie."

"Who are these people who think they have Spike?"

"They're an older couple, in a pretty ritzy section of Palm Springs. Their granddaughter saw one of the posters in Los Angeles and told them about Spike. They claim he's an altered male, gray tabby, and looks just like Spike."

"Don't we have to go see three more people?"

"Yeah. One is a student at College of the Desert. He found the cat sniffing around his garbage. Claims he's a dead ringer for Spike. And the other is a bartender at T.G.I.F. She was getting off work and found the cat out by the dumpster."

"So we should get off to an early start."

"We can sleep in a little. I made the appointments for the afternoon. I thought we could get up late, go out for breakfast, stop by and see some friends of mine. You might even want to do some more shopping."

"I can just get more clothes when we head back to Los Angeles."

"We aren't going back that way. If none of these cats turn out to be Spike, our next stop is Huntington Beach. This guy thinks he has Spike. He lives right on the water and has three cats. He keeps his back window open so they can come and go as they please, and he claims this tabby followed his three right through the open window and started eating their cat food.''

''What do you think?''

''Of all the stories I've heard, that sounds the most like Spike. He doesn't have the personality of a cat who'd hang out by a dumpster. He'd go through the window.''

They floated in silence for a while, then Kevin began to swim easily through the water, back and forth the length of the pool. Gillian couldn't resist sneaking peeks at him.

She sensed he liked being active, didn't regard exercise as something that had to be done. Gillian grimaced as she thought about all the exercise she had had in the previous months. About as close as she got to getting up any steam at all was when Maddie announced she was going to go downstairs and around the corner to the local gourmet donut shop. Then, Gillian would race for her purse and make sure to get in her request before Maddie left.

Swimming? She couldn't remember the last time she'd been in a pool. One of her girlfriends had persuaded her to join a local health club. She'd attended. All of two times. It all boiled down to time and the fact that she never had enough of it.

''Ready for the Jacuzzi? It'll feel good after being in the Jeep most of the day.''

In answer, she rolled onto her stomach and began to dog-paddle toward the shallow end. Esther Williams, she wasn't.

Once inside the Jacuzzi, Gillian made a conscious effort not to let her legs bump Kevin's.

"It's beautiful out tonight," he remarked.

She nodded. "I never get over how clear it is. The way you can see the stars."

"The way it smells after the rain." Kevin tilted back his head and let out a long sigh of appreciation as the hot water bubbled around them. Steam rose up into the dark sky, illuminated by the underwater lights in the Jacuzzi.

Gillian studied him while his eyes were closed. How was it possible that in the space of several hours he was beginning to look so much more attractive to her? His body was muscled, but he didn't look like a weight lifter. A healthy amount of dark blond hair covered his chest, arrowing down to his boxer-style swimming trunks. His shoulders looked...*strong*. She'd already felt the strength in them and in his hands when he'd restrained her by the side of the highway.

Suddenly she was ashamed of her earlier behavior. Ashamed of her swift, unflattering assessment of him. This man was no dumb jock. He simply found a lot of joy in his body. There was so much *life* to Kevin, he wasn't at all like any of the people she knew in the advertising world.

"I'm sorry I was so stupid about my clothes," she said softly.

When he didn't answer right away, she wondered if he'd heard her.

"I'm sorry about the things I said about you in Ben's office. I was...wrong to make that fast a judgment when I didn't even know you."

His head came up, his eyes opened and that grin lit up his entire face.

"I knew this would happen."

"What?"

"I knew we'd have to get along if we spent all our time together."

There was a pause before Gillian said, "I really am sorry."

"Apology accepted." There was a flash of regret in his blue eyes, then he said, "I'm sorry I ever said any of those things in the Jeep earlier. I don't know, I guess I was angry because you...didn't like me."

"I like you now. Or at least I'm starting to."

His leg hit hers gently, accidently, and Gillian instantly pulled hers back.

"That's not entirely true. I was angry because you'd really gotten to me at that party and then I couldn't understand why you looked at me the way you did. And then I did get ticked when I heard you telling Ben you didn't think I was that smart. When we started out on this trip, I had some pretty vivid fantasies about ways I was going to make you pay for that remark."

"What changed your mind?" she asked, curious now.

He smiled, his eyes meeting hers. "You just looked so forlorn and helpless when you sat down on the side of the highway with that smashed suitcase and started to cry. I couldn't continue to be mad at you then."

"Even when I yelled at you?"

"Even then. I know you didn't want to come on this whole chase—"

"Well, now I'm having a pretty good time—"

"And then when all your clothes were ruined and you got so upset—"

"Pretty stupid, huh?"

"Hey, everyone's entitled to feel what they feel. But it just got to me, seeing you sitting in the road like that."

They were silent for a time, listening to the bubbling of the water, smelling the pungent smell of chlorine. The complex was quiet. Most of the condominiums were empty; they were used on weekends. Now, during the middle of the week, the area seemed deserted. The pool-and-Jacuzzi area was completely surrounded by condominiums, and they were set back from the main road.

They were all alone in the world.

Kevin's question broke the silence.

"What did you really want to do, Gillie?"

"What do you mean?"

"Besides advertising. Wasn't there something else you wanted to do?"

"I'm doing just fine with my job. I'm happy enough."

"Happy enough isn't happy."

She could feel herself getting upset, the emotion sweeping through her body, tightening her stomach, tensing her entire body.

"You know, I might have said some pretty stupid things about you, Kevin, but there's something... some attitude you have that makes me feel like I just don't quite measure up in your eyes."

"I think you're just fine. I just wonder why someone like you would choose to be locked up in an office all day long."

"We can't all live lives of high adventure. It's not a very practical way to look at life."

"Who put those words in your mouth?"

She opened her mouth, about to say the words, then shut it. Practicality had been the party line in her family as long as she could remember. First from her father, then her brothers, then finally Bryant. It was funny how she could never really remember her mother having had any opinion at all. Maybe she'd simply been overwhelmed by all the strong-willed men in the family.

"Nobody put those words in my mouth."

"They didn't just materialize out of thin air."

"Can we drop this?"

He hesitated, then nodded.

Once back in her bedroom, Gillian took a quick shower, then combed out her hair and began preparing for bed. She could faintly hear Kevin moving around in the other bedroom.

What was it he wanted from her? Was she an amusement to him, a corporate type he found comical? He obviously hadn't chosen to live his life in the normal nine-to-five vein, that was obvious. Why couldn't he leave her and the choices she'd made alone?

The knock on the door was soft, almost as if he wasn't sure if she were asleep or not.

"Come in."

She was surprised when Kevin entered, a beautifully wrapped present in his hands. The tabby kitten was perched on his shoulder, and when he paused inside her doorway, the kitten began to lick his ear.

"I got you this today when I was shopping. Most of the other stuff I bought was pretty functional, but this... I just thought you should have something pretty to replace everything you lost."

She wouldn't have expected this from him, could barely even believe it now.

"Thank you." He handed her the box, and she took it from him, then continued to look up at him.

"You can open it now, if you like."

He wanted her to. Her fingers strangely clumsy, she untied the elaborate silk ribbon and peeled the tape off the delicate, lacy wrapping paper. Gillian always took her time unwrapping gifts. She'd never wanted for anything material while she'd lived in her father's house, but presents specifically picked out with her true preferences in mind had been rare. She knew most of them had been picked out by her father's secretary and mailed to her boarding school or to the house.

A present from Kevin. As she lifted the lid of the box, she knew it would simply help another piece of the puzzle she knew as Kevin MacClaine fall into place.

But she wasn't prepared for the robe.

It was beautiful. Emerald green silk, simply cut, rich and sumptuous and not at all what she had thought it might be. That he had thought of her when he'd picked it out pleased her immensely.

"Can I try it on?" she asked, her voice almost a whisper.

He laughed then. "It's yours. You can put it on and jump into the pool if you want to—"

But she was already headed for the bathroom. She'd been wearing Ashley's terry robe. Kevin had forgotten pajamas of any kind and she'd been planning on simply wearing the T-shirt over a pair of panties. Now, Ashley's heavy robe fell to the floor as she belted the sash of vivid green around her waist.

It felt glorious against her skin, so light and silky. Gillian lifted her hair out from the collar of the robe, looked at it every which way in the bathroom mirror, then danced out to show it to Kevin.

"I love it!"

"I'm glad. It suits you."

"Thank you." Before she considered the impulse further, she stepped in front of him, placed her hands on his shoulders, raised herself up on tiptoe and kissed him.

It was a swift kiss, and he hadn't been expecting it. She could tell from the startled expression in his eyes as she stepped back.

"I've never had a more beautiful robe," she said, partly to fill the silence and partly because the feelings flooding her were confusing.

"I'm glad you like it," he replied, then turned, balancing the kitten on his shoulder with his hand, and walked out her bedroom door toward his.

WHY DID SHE KISS ME?

Just a simple gesture. A thank-you. Why had it been so awkward right afterward?

He'd sensed it, sensed she'd been as surprised by the spontaneous gesture as he'd been.

But it felt right.

He was warming up to her, no doubt about that. This morning, after what he'd heard in Ben's office, he'd felt like looking Ben directly in the eye and telling him what he could do with his little trip. But the bottom line was, he had to find Spike. So he'd agreed to go, deciding that Miss Gillian Sommers was going to prove to be a royal pain in the behind.

He'd counted on her being a prima donna.

Her vulnerability was something he hadn't thought she would let him see.

Now he wasn't really sure what he was going to do.

Strangely enough, he had the feeling Spike was all right. Though the guy in Huntington Beach had the cat that sounded the most like Spike, Kevin wasn't really convinced any of them were the cat they were looking for.

Something screwy was definitely going on.

Who'd helped her become the practical woman she was? Who had squeezed all the life out of her? He almost wished he'd asked Ben a little more about her, but he'd sensed in Benjamin Merrill a loyalty and caring toward Gillian that might have precluded him spilling her secrets.

He'd just have to find out on his own.

He closed his eyes and tried to relax. Though the Jacuzzi had soothed him, Gillian's unexpected kiss had stirred him right back up. If he'd thought he could have gotten away with it, he would have taken her into his arms and really kissed her. But something in those eyes . . .

There's unhappiness there. And something else. . . .

He rolled over in bed and punched the soft pillow.

Spike, wherever you are, I hope you're having a better time than I am.

THE LARGE TABBY CAT LAY on the soft quilt. Moonlight spilled over the double bed, illuminating the small lump in the center, the fine strands of silvery-gray hair on the feather pillow.

He looked around the bedroom, his pupils large in the darkness. The room smelled safe, he sensed nothing would hurt him here. The old woman was kind; she'd been nothing but kind since she'd found him. The pain had stopped, he was warm and safe, and that was all he could sense right now.

She'd lifted him up on the bed, the soft quilt had felt good against his battered body. She'd fed him pieces of food by hand, petted him, talked to him. There was no one else in the small apartment.

He rubbed the side of his head against the quilt, marking it as his. He would choose to share the bed with the old woman. She was kind, not like the men who had put him in the dark box, then thrown him from the fast car.

Spike yawned, tired after the long day. He'd been thrown from the car window as the two men sped down the freeway, but despite the pain in his leg, Spike had managed to dart across two lanes and into the ivy growing by the ramp. He'd slunk into the bushes once he was off the freeway entirely, dragging his useless leg behind him.

He'd been heading toward home when exhaustion had claimed him. Lying beneath the bushes, he'd thought about just giving up. The leg had hurt him, and he'd given a small cry.

The old woman had answered.

She smelled like the lilacs outside her small apartment. Her touch was gentle and soft, the expression in her eyes was kind.

For now, he knew he could rest here.

Moving gingerly, Spike dragged himself along the bedcover until he was curled up against the old woman. Slowly, cautiously, he laid his head against the old woman's arm and began to purr, deep rumbling sounds that came from his chest.

"Diana?" The name was barely a whisper, and Spike started, aware he had woken her.

"Diana?" The blue eyes were faded with age, and it took her a moment to realize where she was.

"Oh, it's you." Her head turned toward him on the lace-edged pillow, and now he saw the faint stirrings of a smile.

He meowed, to let her know he was listening.

"You just want a little company, hmm?" Now the gentle touch rubbed the top of his head, now beneath his jaw.

Spike purred and closed his eyes, leaning into her.

"All right, all right," the voice murmured, and Spike decided he would stay for a while.

GILLIAN LAY IN BED, fighting the pain.

She knew it would happen tonight. Too much had happened; it was all so different from her usual routine. Unpredictability always scared her, gave her the feeling her life was totally out of control.

She hadn't felt safe for a long time.

She got up slowly, made her way toward the boxes and bags lying on the carpeted floor. Somewhere, amid all the clothes Kevin had brought back, was the bag from the drugstore. Thank God all of that stuff hadn't been in her big suitcase.

She found the bottle of Pepto Bismol, unscrewed the cap and put it to her lips.

Several swallows later, she recapped it, then lay down on the floor, curled up in the fetal position, her hands against her stomach.

There was nothing to do but wait it out.

HE HEARD THE NOISE IN THE HALLWAY. Kevin stopped breathing and listened.

Gillian was up. Restless. And in the main bathroom. She'd given him the master bedroom with connecting bath, so that the kitten's litter box could go in the bathroom.

He started to breathe again, but still listened.

The kitten, awakened by the tension in his body, meowed softly and jumped off the bed. Kevin followed the little animal with his eyes as she headed straight for the bathroom Gillian occupied and slipped inside.

He got up out of bed, his mind made up.

"Gillie?" Kevin knocked softly on the bathroom door. Though the door was slightly ajar, he wanted to respect her privacy.

"Oh, please go away."

It took him a second before he realized she was talking to Junior. She'd sounded as if she were in pain.

Not hesitating, Kevin opened the door and stepped inside the bathroom.

She was lying in the bathtub, in her T-shirt and underwear, her cheek against the white porcelain. Her vivid, coppery hair was a sharp contrast to the black-and-white decor. Junior, inquisitive as always, was batting at her hair.

Kevin swept up the kitten and hunkered down on to the floor, so he could see Gillian more easily.

"Gillie? Is it your stomach?" She was curled up slightly, her hands pressed against her abdomen.

She nodded.

"What can I do?"

"Nothing. It's…happened before. If I just…wait, it gets better."

Her face was sickly pale, he could see a fine sheen of sweat on her forehead. Having dealt with numerous animals in pain, he was attuned to the subtle signs of intense pain in someone who didn't want to admit that was what was going on.

Her legs started to shake, and Kevin reached up for a dry, fluffy bath sheet. Doubling it, he tucked it gently over her legs. Then he got up just long enough to turn on the heater, returning instantly to her side.

"Hold my hand," he said, reaching for hers.

She hesitated for just an instant, then took it.

"Go ahead and squeeze," he told her calmly.

Her slender fingers and slight body belied a strength he hadn't known she possessed. She gripped his hand tightly, closed her eyes and battled with the pain.

"Try to breathe, Gillie. It helps. Come on, breathe with me."

She took a deep breath, then exhaled a sob.

"I'm taking you to the hospital."

"No! No...it gets better. It's getting better."

"Have you had your appendix out?"

She nodded her head. "It's...stomach. It's okay."

It's okay.

The thought haunted him long after the pain had abated and he'd carried her to her room and tucked her into her bed.

It's okay.

To be in such pain. To live such a joyless life. To want so badly to break free but have absolutely no idea how to do it.

It's okay.

He made up his mind in an instant. Even though it was after three in the morning, he picked up the phone and dialed Benjamin Merrill's home number.

Ben answered on the fourth ring.

"What's with Gillie's stomach?" he asked. He didn't want to waste his time or Merrill's.

"Is she all right?"

"Barely. I just put her to bed."

"I think it's an ulcer."

"Has she seen a doctor?"

"She claims she doesn't have the time."

"Is something wrong at work? Anything that would be putting her under stress?"

"Just Spike." Ben paused. "Or being with you."

Kevin hadn't thought of that, and he didn't like Merrill catching him off guard with the idea.

"We've been getting along."

"I thought you would. This trip could be the best thing for her. Let her relax a little, reassess things."

Something, the little niggling thought that this trip was not all it seemed to be on the surface, clicked on in Kevin's brain.

"So you wanted her out of the office."

"I'm worried about her. She's needed to take a vacation for some time. God knows she had the time coming."

"So we're not really looking for Spike, are we?"

"Let me put it this way. You could have easily done the job yourself. I wanted to get Gillie out of the office and give her a chance to relax. There is absolutely nothing here she has to concern herself with. I'm just hoping you can show her a good time."

"What exactly does this good time entail?"

"Whatever you want it to. You could do worse than Gillie."

Kevin had to grin. "A little corporate matchmaking, huh?" He liked Ben Merrill, the man was street-smart, solid and dependable. He'd made sure the Kitty Krunchies deal was both lucrative and fair.

"You could say that."

"Good. Thanks. I may just take you up on it." He changed the subject, all business now. "Has she ever been to a doctor about this?"

"Once. He suggested she slow down and take a serious look at her life-style. I think he even gave her a prescription. She threw it away and decided to try and go the over-the-counter route."

"She doesn't want to admit anything's wrong with her."

"Right. Thinks she's invincible, just like her old man did." There was regret in Ben's voice, and Kevin wondered how well he'd known Gillie's father.

"I get it. If she admits nothing is wrong, she can pretend nothing is wrong."

"Exactly."

"Okay. Thanks, Ben. Is it all right if I call you from time to time? I mean about Gillie."

He could almost hear Ben's smile over the phone. "Anytime."

GILLIAN CAME AWAKE SLOWLY, glancing around the unfamiliar bedroom. For just a second she didn't know where she was, then the events of the past day washed over her, causing her to pull the pillow over her head.

As soon as she moved, Junior came awake. The kitten climbed on her back and walked slowly up her spine, then began to lick her hair.

"Stop it," she muttered. But she didn't even have the heart to swat the little feline off the bed.

Twenty-four hours. In twenty-four hours she'd insulted Kevin, told him off, listened as he told her off, eaten two meals with this man, completely lost her mind out on a rainy stretch of highway, let him go to the local mall and buy her clothing, gone swimming and into the Jacuzzi with him...

And had a sick stomach in a T-shirt and pair of underwear, all the while holding his hand.

And wanted him to kiss her.

And kissed him.

Twenty-four hours.

A true woman of mystery.

This can't be happening to me.

As if in answer to her question, the man who had been uppermost in her thoughts pushed the bedroom door open and sauntered in carrying a tray.

"I thought you might be up by now."

"What time is it?" she asked, sitting up and swinging her legs over the side of the bed.

"Stay." He set the tray down on the end table by the bed.

"What?"

"Sorry. Habit. Don't get out of bed yet."

She looked at him, puzzled. "What time is it?"

"Half past noon."

"Noon! We've got to get going!"

"No we don't. I did some calling and switched our appointments around. I already went out and talked to that college guy—"

"We're *supposed* to be doing this together—"

"And it wasn't Spike."

On cue, an enormous long-haired calico cat sauntered into the bedroom. Junior trilled a tiny little meow and leaped down from the bed to prance in front of the bigger cat.

The calico simply ignored her.

"Didn't he want to keep it?" Gillian asked, eyeing the big cat.

"A college guy? He's sharing a one-bedroom apartment with two other guys. Party central. Anyway, it's spring break, and these guys have other things on their mind besides cats."

"What about the older couple?"

"I saw them right after Mr. College. It wasn't Spike, and they were delighted. He was pretty close, though. He looked just like him. This cat's got it made, they're both crazy about him. The old guy found him walking along the road and took him home. That cat's already running the place."

"I suppose you've seen the bartender."

"Now *that* kitten was a honey. He wasn't really a tabby, he was more a tortoiseshell. Cute little thing. She wanted to keep him, so that one was another happy ending."

"But we're no closer to finding Spike."

"True. I called the home office, and Ben told me to tell you to stay put for today—"

"You told him about last night?"

"I told him nothing. The guy in Huntington Beach is out of town until the day after tomorrow, so there's no use busting our butts getting over there until we can see the cat."

"You have a remarkably blasé attitude about Spike."

He smiled down at her. "Call it intuition. I have a feeling Spike's just fine, wherever he is. Now, eat your breakfast."

She eyed the tray suspiciously. "I never eat breakfast."

"After I worked so hard? Ah, try it, you might like it."

"What is it?"

"You've never had corn flakes with milk and sliced bananas? Gillie, you haven't lived. Breakfast is my favorite meal of the day."

"Bring the tray over." She admitted defeat.

He settled the tray in her lap, deftly poured the cornflakes, then sliced half a banana over the cereal.

"You went to the market this morning, too?"

"Only for a few necessities." He poured milk over the corn flakes, slid a spoon into the bowl and leaned back on his elbows. "Have you ever been to the Jensen's out here?"

"No." She picked up the spoon and eyed the cereal.

"We'll have to go before we leave. It's like the Disneyland of markets, you'll love it."

"I don't like Disneyland."

Now he looked truly wounded. "Gillie, you astonish me. How can you not like Disneyland?"

"It's boring."

"It's fun—ah, I see."

"What?" she mumbled, her mouth full of corn flakes.

"You need a crash course in fun. And what a lucky coincidence—"

"You're just the man to teach me. MacClaine, count yourself lucky I'm eating this breakfast and don't push your luck—"

"You're right, we'll save Disneyland for another day."

She finished breakfast, then took a shower as both Junior and Big Calico attempted to get in the large stall with her. Dressing quickly, Gillie pulled on a pair of jeans and a white tank top. Slipping on her thongs, she quickly braided her hair down her back in a fat braid, then walked out into the living room, both cats hot on her heels.

"So what are we doing today?"

"Let's take a cruise through town, see some old buddies of mine, then stop at the market on the way back. We can lie by the pool for an hour or two, then go out for dinner and maybe a movie."

"This sound suspiciously like a vacation."

He grinned. "Try to be open-minded."

KEVIN'S "OLD BUDDIES" turned out to be a married couple in their fifties. Gil and Lynne ran the Shakey's on the corner of Bob Hope Drive and Highway 111. Before Gillian quite knew what had happened, they were sitting outside on the patio with a pitcher of beer, though Lynne opted for a Cherry Coke.

"So you're sure I can't talk you into two more cats," Kevin teased.

Lynne, a petite brunette with sparkling brown eyes and shoulder-length hair, turned mischievous eyes on her husband. "What do you think, Gil?"

Gil simply glowered. He was quite good at it, too, with his bushy brows and piercing eyes. But Gillian soon learned that his wry wit covered a soft heart.

"Gato would throw a fit!" Gil said. "That would be it, she'd leave."

"How is Gato?" Kevin was completely relaxed, sitting back in his chair. Gillian had expected his buddies to be men about his age, and she hadn't looked forward to this meeting. She'd been sure she was going to feel left out. But Gil and Lynne were warm people, and the conversation flowed easily, sparked with laughter.

"Fat as a pig. She eats the meal I feed her, then goes across to the next trailer and eats another meal with Tiki."

"Tiki is Carol's cat," Kevin explained to Gillian. "And Carol's the Saint Francis of Mahoney's Trailer Park. She takes in all the stray cats and dogs."

"She makes you look like an amateur, Kevin," Gil said. "You still have that pig?"

"Clementine? She got a call last month for an Isuzu commercial."

Gil snorted. "A pig in a commercial."

"Now, Gil! Kevin, call us and let us know when it comes on television."

They visited with Gil and Lynne for about two hours, the conversation interrupted as one or the other of the couple had to check on how things were coming along in the pizza parlor. Lynne was the more talkative of the two, and Gillian felt herself being skillfully drawn out. Lynne was fascinated by her career, and by the time they said their goodbyes, Gillian felt as if she had known the couple for a long time.

"Now, Gil, just keep the door unlocked and we'll drop those two cats off on our way out."

"Kevin, you'll drop more than those cats if I catch you." Gil turned to Gillian. "You're traveling with this guy?"

Gillian laughed. "No more cats in the trailer park, I promise."

She felt strangely bereft as she watched Kevin shake Gil's hand and get a warm hug from Lynne. Then Lynne surprised Gillian by turning around and hugging her.

"You two be careful on the road. The traffic is crazy out there," Lynne warned them as they left.

"That's right! Spring break, Gil, your favorite time of year."

Gil simply glowered as Lynne took his arm.

"Come on, Magoo, let's get back and make some more pizzas."

They were driving down 111 when Gillian asked, "Why did she call him Magoo?"

Kevin glanced at her quickly, then back at the road. "Gil's legally blind. They've always had to write up the orders pretty big so he can see them. But he's still the best manager around. They're a real team, those two."

Gillian looked out at the mountains as she absorbed this and thought of her mother and father. Never, in the entire time she had seen them together, had she felt even a little of the warmth Gil and Lynne seemed to radiate so effortlessly.

"You've known them long?"

"They're my second parents. They've helped me through some difficult decisions. Sometimes I think your own parents are too close. It helps to talk to someone who doesn't see you as their son or daughter."

She thought of Ben and all he'd done for her, but Gillian remained silent as Kevin continued to drive.

JENSEN'S WAS TRULY UNBELIEVABLE. There wasn't a can or jar out of place. The produce looked too beautiful to be real. The market also included a bakery with a row of small booths and tables, and the smell of freshly ground coffee tantalized Gillian as they walked through the gleaming glass doors.

"Nice place, huh? And you would've missed it."

She had to admit it was like no other supermarket she'd ever seen. The selection in the deli department, the various meats and salads, put a fine restaurant to shame.

"We could just pick up something from the deli and call it an early night," she suggested. Gillian was intimately acquainted with the salad bar at her local market.

"Where's your sense of adventure? Besides, as late as you slept, we should be able to stay out all night. It'll be your first spring break in Palm Springs."

"I'm not that sure I want to participate."

"Leave it to me."

They were almost out of the market when Gillian said, "Wait, I want to check out the cat-food aisle. See how Kitty Krunchies is doing."

Kevin hesitated, then followed her.

There were several shoppers in the pet-food section and Gillian noticed a woman in her forties filling her cart with expensive, canned cat food. This was the kind of cat-food consumer the Kitty Krunchies Kat Food Company loved to convert.

"Excuse me," she said, walking up to the woman. "I just adopted a cat from the local shelter and I was wondering if you could recommend a good cat food."

The woman took the bait. "This is the best." She indicated the cans in her cart.

"I don't have a lot of money," Gillian continued. "I notice this Krunchies stuff is marked down. Is it any good?"

"I think they should throw it all away! I tried that brand, and Bosco and Bluto had a terrible reaction to it! After they refused to eat for three days, I gave in and threw it all away—I didn't even dare try to foist it off on my neighbors!"

Shaken, Gillian smiled and picked up a couple of the expensive individual cans with the pop tops. The woman smiled back and wheeled her cart away.

Gillian was about to put the cans back on the shelf when another woman touched her arm.

"I have to agree with her, dear. When I gave that Krunchies stuff to my Bear and my Fritz, they went on a hunger strike, the poor little dears. I had to fry them up some ground turkey before they forgave me."

"It's terrible stuff!" chimed in a white-haired man in a navy jogging suit. "Sent the wife to pick up some cat food one night and she brought it home. Said, 'Well, George, it was the cheapest on the shelf.' But our Mitzi wouldn't touch the stuff. I don't know how that Spike eats it. He's a tough guy, that cat."

After the customers wheeled their carts way down the aisle, Gillian looked at Kevin.

"Well, Spike eats it."

"They put ground sirloin in the bottom of the dish."

"Have you ever fed Spike any of the free cat food the company sent you?"

He looked vaguely guilty. "He wouldn't touch the stuff. But you know, Gillie, it's only gotten really bad in the last year and a half. Before that, Spike liked it fine. I think they started trying to cut corners and that's when they screwed it up."

She nodded her head. "Wonderful. The biggest account I ever got the agency is for a cat food most people wouldn't feed to their dog."

"You've got to look on the bright side, Gillie. My sister says it makes great compost."

Chapter Five

"Come on, Junior, at least try it."

The kitten eyed the bowl filled with Kitty Krunchies, then stared back up at Gillian with wide green eyes. She meowed, her pink mouth opening wide, the sound plaintive.

"Cut that out. Just try it."

In answer, the kitten scooped a piece of the kibble out of the dish and began to bat it around the kitchen floor. Big Calico walked up to the bowl, sniffed it, then sauntered away in the opposite direction.

Gillian had bought a small box of Kitty Krunchies, despite Kevin's argument against it. He'd told her he already had plenty of cat food for the two cats and any others they might pick up in their search for Spike. But something had compelled her to test the food for herself.

This was the absolute last time she accepted anyone else's word on a product. She hadn't thought of testing Kitty Krunchies. After all, it wasn't as if she could try it herself. But she should have borrowed someone's cat and given the food a test run.

And so far, in this test run, both Junior and Big Calico had given Kitty Krunchies a rating. A bit fat F.

For failure.

"It really is bad stuff," she said as Kevin came into the kitchen in his bathing suit, a towel draped around his neck.

"These guys weren't exactly educated at the *Cordon Bleu*."

"But they know what they like." Gillian picked up the bowl and dumped its contents into the trash bag.

"So it's bad food. It didn't start out that way, maybe the company can get it together and improve the product."

"Did Spike really eat it in the beginning?"

Kevin looked sheepish. "He's kind of spoiled. He likes wet food. I figure it's a small thing, giving him the food he likes. After he started making money for the compound in a big way, I put him on one of those fancy veterinarian's diets, the food you buy in pet stores. The stuff that's good for you. He hated that, too. Spike is the kind of guy who would eat every meal at Jack in the Box if he could. He likes fast-food cat food, the stuff that tastes great."

"What does he eat?"

When Kevin named Kitty Krunchies's major rival, Gillian silently admitted complete defeat.

"Come on, don't look like that. We still have time to catch a couple of hours of sun. There's a great pool waiting out there, and we have the place practically to ourselves. What more could you want?"

"A good-tasting cat food."

He grinned. "Get your suit on."

SHE HAD TO ADMIT IT. She was having fun.

She and Kevin lay out by the pool, rubbed on sun-tan lotion, listened to the radio. Occasionally one of them would run up and get some soda or juice or a bag of corn chips.

They lazed the time away. Gillian lay down on a chaise longue and watched Kevin swim. He was so...*active*. She wondered if he thought she was a lazy slug, then found herself rejecting the notion. One thing Kevin MacClaine wasn't was judgmental.

He came back out of the water, dripping wet, then grabbed his towel and began to rub his hair dry.

"What's your favorite kind of food? Besides sushi."

"Chinese."

"Szechuan?"

"Fine."

"Szechuan it is. They have some great restaurants out here. When we go back inside, I'll call for reservations and we can get cleaned up and go eat."

"It doesn't have to be anything fancy—"

"It's spring break. I'll call and make sure we have a restaurant to go to. Even with reservations, the wait will be longer than usual."

Gillian thought of the small amount of clothing she had to choose from. "I don't have anything to wear."

"That's no excuse. We'll stop at the mall on the way to dinner. I'll make sure we have enough time."

"You don't take no for an answer, do you?"

"Not most of the time."

The dress she bought was simple and stunning, tur-quoise with a halter top and full skirt. Gillian also bought a pair of sandals, then dressed in one of the store's dressing rooms.

It *was* a pretty dress. Typical of most of the clothing seen in the desert resort area, it was casual and stylish. The sun this afternoon had given her a bit of a glow, and now, her hair gleaming and falling loose around her shoulders and just a touch of makeup on her eyes and lips, she felt she was staring into the mirror at a stranger.

Unbidden, the image of Kathleen Turner in *Romancing the Stone* came into her mind. The scene in which she was dancing in the courtyard with Michael Douglas in the gauzy blouse and skirt.

And the scene in the cave where they found the stone, where Joan Wilder told Jack Colter he was the best time she'd ever had in her life.

The woman who looked back at her in the dressing-room mirror did *not* look like a stuffed shirt. She looked like a woman who was vibrant and happy, sparkling and alive.

Even though her client's cat food was the worst in the world.

Stop it. Just let yourself have a good time. For once. Until we find Spike.

Kevin MacClaine was such a puzzle.

And he frightened her to death.

He'd carried her to bed. Tucked her in. Held her hand while she was in pain. In little more than a day, he'd shown more genuine affection toward her than her family had in a lifetime.

She thought of the somber, achingly formal dinners in the dining room of the San Francisco house.

Courses being placed on the gleaming wooden table, other courses being silently taken away. Minimalist conversation. Mostly about business. Important, *practical* matters. As a child she'd sensed her place was to be seen, never heard.

She'd certainly never laughed.

The saleslady rapped lightly on the door. "Excuse me. Your boyfriend told me to tell you that if you want to make your reservation, you'd better hurry."

"What did he really say?" She smiled.

There was a hint of laughter in the woman's voice. "Find out if she died in there."

"I thought so. Tell him I'll be right out."

As the saleslady's steps faded away on the carpet, Gillian gave her reflection one last look.

Go out there and have a really good time. See what it's like. He's certainly different from Bryant....

Picking up her purse and the clothes she'd been wearing when she came in, Gillian left the dressing room.

KEVIN WAS A WONDERFUL dinner companion. He kept her laughing over their meal with stories about his escapades with his animals in the world of show business. And Gillian, as she egged him on, asking questions and laughing, wondered why Samantha ever let this man out of her sight.

Their food was exquisite. They ended up ordering three entrees, then sharing the chicken with red peppers and cashews, fresh crab with Peking sauce and duck with fresh ginger and green pepper.

"So this friend of mine had this rabbit," Kevin continued. "And he spoiled it rotten. Anyway, this rabbit knew she had the upper hand. He lived in this apartment complex in Hollywood."

"What was he doing with a rabbit? A dog, I can see, but what man wants a pet rabbit?"

"He'd given it to his kids when he saw them over Easter. Mark's divorced. Anyway, when his ex knew she was the one who was going to end up cleaning the cage every week, she told him to come and get his rabbit out of there."

"And?"

"So, when he finally realized he was going to have to clean the cage, he called me and asked me what to do. I told him how to do it, but what Mark hadn't told me was that he'd never actually handled this rabbit. He'd given it to his kids when it was tiny, in a cardboard box. I guess the kids weren't really gentle with the bunny. Mark moved her to his apartment in the cage, and he'd been setting food inside the cage, filling the water bottle and petting her while she ate. He thought picking her up would be a piece of cake."

"So why did he end up getting involved with the police?"

"Have you ever heard a rabbit scream?"

"No."

"It sounds just like a woman. It's this cry they let out when they're convinced their life is in danger."

"And this rabbit screamed when Mark picked her up? That seems a little extreme."

"You'd scream, too, if you'd been handled by those kids. Anyway, Mark panicked. The way he tells the story he was racing around the apartment holding on to this struggling, screaming rabbit. Three of his neighbors thought he was murdering one of his girlfriends, and when the police showed up, he dropped the bunny and they all had to go chasing through his apartment to catch it. He called me when it was all over and the bunny was back in her cage.''

''And?''

''Offered me a thousand dollars if I'd take the rabbit and get it out of his life.''

''Did you take her?''

''Honey's fine. She gets a lot of work in commercials around Easter time.''

''Poor Mark.''

''Yeah, it was pretty awful.'' Kevin started to laugh. ''Sam was over at the house when Mark called, and after I hung up and told her the story we laughed until we cried.''

She'd forgotten about Samantha, girlfriend guarding the hearth while Kevin was on the road. Gillian looked down at her plate, pretending intense interest in a piece of crab. Then, not knowing what else to do, she decided to say what was on her mind.

''Doesn't she mind, you being on the road with me?''

''Why should she?''

''Do you have one of those open relationships?''

His eyes were sparkling with suppressed mirth. ''No. I never believed in that kind of thing. Even if Sam and I were involved, it would be impossible because Ryan would tear my head off my shoulders in a jealous rage.''

The smile on his face was at odds with his outrageous words.

"And who's Ryan?"

"My cousin. And Sam's husband."

"You and Sam aren't—"

"Nope. Never have been. Never will."

The sudden surge of elation caught Gillian off guard. She set her fork down and clasped her hands in front of her to keep them steady. "So why did you let me believe the two of you were an item?"

"I never said we were."

"You omitted a few things."

"What about Henry? Is this guy really in the picture in a big way?"

She thought of Henry, wagging his fishy tail as he swam along the side of the immense glass bowl he called home.

"No. He was never really in the running."

"Now we're getting somewhere."

"Kevin—"

"In my vast experience with the opposite sex, I've come to the conclusion that women are a lot like rabbits."

"You touch them and they scream?"

"No, no. Mark's was an exceptional case. What I'm saying is that rabbits are extremely vulnerable creatures. If they even see a shadow brush by their cages, they head for their burrows. They don't have that many ways to protect themselves against getting hurt. But they still come out of that burrow every day. I think it's a lot like that for a woman in love."

"What about men?"

He smiled. "Some of the men I know remind me of buffalos on the make. I think women are more vulnerable because they usually have more to lose."

"Like what?"

"Like...innocence."

"You mean virginity?"

"It's more than that. You see a man who's been through the trenches and he'll put on a big act that nothing really got to him. He broke up with her, right? He's going to be all right even if it kills him to keep it all inside. But these same men—and this is a statistical fact—are the ones who stay home night after night with the blinds pulled."

"And the women?"

"They're out there looking. They're tough. They don't give up. They're out there going to parties and talking to people in grocery lines and doing whatever has to be done because that urge to really merge with a man is that strong."

"So you look on women as the superior sex?"

"You can't have any knowledge of biology and believe otherwise. Let me put it this way. We went through men's physiology in a day and a half. It took over a month to cover everything in a woman's system. It's a miracle."

"You really believe that?"

He leaned forward, his eyes intent. "I do. I think men are pretty terrific, but we pale in comparison with you guys. You know, Ryan came by my house right after Sam had Johanna. He'd been in the delivery room with her and caught the baby. He said he never knew what strength was until he saw what she had to go through to give birth.

"He caught Johanna. He even cut the cord. But he said for most of it he felt like a bystander. Sam was pretty cool about the whole thing, and I know she needed Ryan there, but in the end, she was the one who did it. Tell me if you can think of anything much more remarkable than having a baby."

Gillian felt immensely vulnerable, and decided to argue with him. "Anyone can have a baby. It's raising that baby into a halfway decent child that takes talent."

"You're right. And women do most of that, too, and don't get much credit for it. We keep paying all this lip service to women and children, but we don't really treat them very well."

"Women are the top consumers in this country. Most of the advertising is geared toward them."

"And most of it's spent making them feel they aren't good enough. Making them feel they have to have whiter whites, cleaner toilets, floors that sparkle and dishes you can see your face in. I wouldn't call that doing them a favor."

"You really like women."

"Had to. I was outnumbered at home. No, seriously, I used to watch what my sisters went through, and I couldn't believe the fighting they had to do to be taken seriously. I worry about Kelly all the time. Rock-and-roll is still a male bastion, and if she isn't careful, they'll grind her up and spit her out."

They talked on into the night, until they both realized the crowd was thinning and the employees in the restaurant wanted them out so they could clean up and go home.

When Kevin reached into his pocket for his wallet, Gillian placed a hand on his arm. "Let me put it on the company credit card."

"Nope. Now you're going to see an example of male bullheadedness and masculine pride. I'll take care of it."

"But—"

"No buts. This is our first date and I'll take care of it."

Everything inside her stilled as she watched Kevin chatting with the waiter as he came back to collect the money. Kevin was different from any man she'd ever known. Perhaps the one quality that was most different was the incredible warmth she sensed within him. He was a warm and accepting man, so unlike what she was used to.

The highway was a madhouse. Trucks, vans and cars crept along, bumper to bumper. The vast majority of the traffic was made up of teenagers and college students. The toy of the moment was the squirt gun, and furious water fights were in progress between the occupants of the various cars.

Most of the young men were dressed in what seemed to be the unspoken uniform, wildly colored shorts and T-shirts. The girls wore swimsuits with nylon shorts over them. Feet were either bare, thonged or sneakered. Hair ranged from the wildest of styles to the most casual.

"So this is spring break," Gillian called above the noise of revving motors and excited laughter.

"You got it. A time for students to cut loose, cram into hotel rooms by the hundreds and get down to some serious partying."

"How can people stand it?"

He gave her a quizzical look, one eyebrow cocked. "Gillie, don't break my heart and tell me you never experienced spring break?"

"Never. I spent my holidays with my family."

"That settles it." He changed lanes, using that quick grin to make sure the women crowded in the car in the other lane let him in front of them.

"Settles what?"

"We've got to hit a few places. It's never too late to make this kind of stuff up. You just have to be cool."

"Kevin, I don't think—"

"That's my girl. Don't think."

THEY HIT SEVERAL BARS, and by the time they were in their fifth of the evening, Gillian had to admit that the excitement was contagious. Spring break was like one big circus. Everywhere they went, people were infected with it. Bartenders and cocktail waitresses outdid themselves, people danced and partied frenetically.

And Gillian found herself right in the middle of it all.

She never would have made it through the evening without Kevin. He managed to find them tables, squeeze them past crowds, ease tension with a smile and the right word.

And now, into her third Tequila Sunrise, Gillian found herself starting to tell him things she never thought she would have said.

"You're really not that bad," she said, her lips against Kevin's ear. "I thought this trip was going to be awful, but it's been kind of fun, except for the beginning."

"It's not over yet."

"Do you still think I'm a stuffed shirt?" She couldn't fathom why, but his answer was terribly important to her.

"Not a chance. I misjudged you totally."

"Kevin, I think that I—"

"Kevin!" The blonde that approached their table was petite and sparkly, with large blue eyes and a curvaceous figure. "How're you doing?"

"Danielle! Gillie, this is Danielle. She's the bartender I was telling you about, the one that ended up keeping the kitten."

Gillian nodded her head, smiling automatically. She didn't know why, but as she watched Danielle's relaxed manner and easy, sexy smile, she felt less and less like a casual party animal and more like the proverbial stuffed shirt.

Kevin was a sociable man. He liked to go out and explore the world, mingle with people, burn the proverbial candle at both ends and the middle.

She was barely a sparkler.

Danielle didn't stay at their small table long, but when she left, Gillian didn't miss the lingering kiss she gave Kevin on his cheek.

They left soon after that.

Gillian didn't say much during the ride home. She kept picturing Kevin and Danielle together. She was the type of woman who would be full of fun, would know how to laugh with a man, hold his interest. Danielle was a lethal combination of stunning blond looks and charm, her social skills probably honed to a fine edge by her bartending.

Gillian stared out the Jeep's window, the dry desert air cool against her flushed face.

What did she care if Danielle was perfect for him? Why was she so upset at the thought of him preferring Danielle over her? They never would have met if it hadn't been for Spike. She still sometimes wondered why Ben had sent her on this trip. The whole thing was so unnerving—she felt safer knowing what was going to happen during the course of the day when it was neatly entered into her leather-bound appointment calendar.

She wasn't really suited to life with Kevin Mac-Claine.

So who asked you if you were. Grow up. He's just being nice to you.

But she knew it was more than that. Sometimes, when she caught him looking at her, it was there, something in those eyes. . . .

He scared her. The thought of their friendship slowly developing into something more was terrifying. She hadn't been enough for Bryant, and if she hadn't been able to please him, there was no possible way she could ever imagine Kevin being happy with her—

Gillian was jarred out of her thoughts by the Jeep turning into the large drive of the condominium complex. She glanced at Kevin, but he seemed intent on his driving. When they reached the parking spaces closest to the path to Ben's condo, she spoke.

"Could you drop me off here? I'm kind of tired."

There were several cars parked by the path. It was nearing the weekend, and they weren't alone in the complex anymore. If Kevin dropped her off, he'd have to drive further to find a parking space.

He stopped the Jeep and didn't say anything, but when she started to open the door, she felt his hand on her arm, his touch gentle.

"What did I do, Gillie?"

"Nothing. I'm just tired, that's all. And these new sandals hurt my feet."

He didn't take his hand away, and she didn't feel right about simply leaping out of the Jeep while he was touching her.

"Are you telling me the truth?" His voice was very soft.

What a strange question. She felt ashamed suddenly, that she should be so rude to this man who had shown her nothing but kindness and laughter.

"Sort of."

"Tell me."

She could feel tears gathering in her eyes as she turned back into the passenger seat, and she kept her vision focused on her hands clasped in her lap.

"I'm not very good at this," she said quietly.

"What?"

"Dating." It took her a moment to get that word out of her mouth, but after all, he had said it was their first date tonight.

She could hear his sigh, then out of the corner of her eye, she saw him lean his head back on the driver's seat.

"You may not think you're very good at dating, but you're very good with people. I had a great time."

"There are too many things—I think I'm too messed up to have a relationship with anyone right now." She took a deep, steadying breath. "I think you're wasting your time."

"Will you trust me to be the judge of that?"

She was silent for a short time, and Kevin took his hand away and turned off the engine.

"Gillie, tell me the real reason."

"I'm afraid."

"Afraid of what?"

"I'm afraid you're going to try and kiss me."

"I'd thought about it. But I won't do it if you don't want me to."

She felt one fat, hot tear run slowly down her face, but she refused to wipe it away.

"I get— You confuse me."

"What confuses you?"

"Why you would want to be with me when—when Danielle would love to go out with you."

"Gillie." His voice was warm, so very warm. "Danielle and I got along really well this morning. She fixed me coffee and we talked for a while, even after I knew she was going to keep the kitten. When I left her apartment, she gave me her phone number and told me she'd love to see me again. But I told her there was already someone I was interested in and it wouldn't be fair to any of us.''

She couldn't speak.

"I won't touch you until you tell me it's okay. Does that make you feel better? I don't mind your being in control of that.''

She nodded her head.

"And if you still want to get out of the Jeep here, that's all right. But just tell me the truth, Gillie. That's all I ask.''

"All right. Can I get out now?''

"Sure.''

Feeling incredibly stupid, she left the Jeep and walked swiftly to the path, then made her way to Ben's condo. Leaving the door unlocked for Kevin, she went into her bedroom and closed the door.

Big Calico was sleeping on the bed, but she raised her head, eyed Gillian and yawned before setting her head back down on the pillow.

Gillian undressed quickly, then eased the cat over and climbed beneath the covers of the bed.

She heard Kevin come in, then heard the lock on the front door clicking into place and the sound of his footsteps as he walked down the hallway toward his bedroom.

And as she closed her eyes and tried to will her tense body to relax, she wondered how she could ever face him in the morning.

IT WAS EASIER than she expected. They spent a quiet day, and Kevin didn't bring up their conversation from the evening before. Gillian washed the sheets and towels they had used, and both of them worked for a short time cleaning the condominium. Then they spent the remainder of the day out by the pool, soaking up the hot desert sun.

It was evening before they loaded the Jeep. As they left the Palm Springs area and turned onto the 10 West, Gillian noticed highway patrolmen at the freeway entrance across from them, the one leading into town.

"They're turning people back. A couple of years ago, the students got out of hand. This year they had it pretty well under control. I don't think they ever want a repeat of last time."

She looked at him, sitting in the driver's seat, and wondered what he was really thinking about last night. She knew Kevin was a strong man, but even strong men had their feelings. And she wondered whether he thought she didn't like him at all.

You did call him some pretty awful things. Gillian felt as if the tiniest part of her reserve was giving way. The one thing she couldn't stand was to make Kevin think she didn't like him.

What was it on that plaque Maddie had hanging by her desk? Something about every journey starting the same way, with a single step.

Slowly, carefully, she reached over and slid her hand into his. His fingers were warm, the skin calloused. She felt his response instantly. His hand tightened over hers, his thumb rubbing the top of her hand.

She squeezed tighter, and he squeezed back.

She didn't dare look at him and kept her eyes on the road as they headed west.

HUNTINGTON BEACH WAS just the right contrast to the desert, with its cool, ocean-scented breezes and miles of sandy beaches. Alan Underwood, the computer consultant with three cats plus, perhaps Spike, agreed to meet them that evening after work. Gillian, in a quieter mood, didn't object when Kevin drove the Jeep into the parking lot of an oceanfront hotel and booked them two rooms.

She thought about taking a nap, then disregarded the idea. Kevin was energy personified, and she knew that whatever he was up for that afternoon, it would be fun.

"Laundry, I think," he said, as soon as they were in their rooms. There was a connecting door that he'd knocked on and opened within minutes after they were settled in.

"I can just go back to my house and get more clothes."

"Nope. The next stop is nowhere near Los Angeles."

She lay back on the large, queen-sized bed and closed her eyes. "I don't suppose you're going to tell me."

"I'm going to surprise you."

Junior and Big Calico had joined her on the bed, and now the kitten was busily trying to bite her on the nose.

"What do you plan to do with all these cats? I mean, what if we go from place to place and all these people think they have Spike but they don't. And if you keep taking these cats along—"

"We'll find them homes."

She opened her eyes and gave him a look. "I think you're getting attached to them."

"Maybe. But you have to admit, I have the room."

She closed her eyes again, only to open them when Kevin announced their agenda once again.

"Laundry. Get your bathing suit on and gather up your clothes."

"My suit?"

He gave her a playfully exasperated look. "Haven't you ever done laundry on a road trip before? If you're lucky enough to be near a beach, you put on your suit, go down by the water and catch some rays while your clothes are cleaning."

"I've never done this before."

"First time for everything."

LAUNDERLAND WAS CLOSE ENOUGH to the beach that they were by the waves within ten minutes of shoving their clothing into washing machines. Kevin had beach towels in the Jeep, and they stopped at an Osco's for sunscreen.

"You'll look like a lobster if you don't get some of this on," Kevin commented as he smoothed the lotion on Gillian's exposed back.

She liked the way his hands felt. His touch was firm and very assured. His fingers massaged the tightness away, and she felt her neck and shoulders relaxing.

"Put some on me, would you?"

His back was to her and she couldn't help but notice the smoothness of his skin, stretched over muscle. She squeezed out a small amount of lotion into her palm, then began to rub it over his back. Kevin sighed and leaned into her touch.

"Nice day to do laundry, isn't it?"

"Yes." Gillian was sure this particular stretch of beach was crowded on the weekends, but as it was a weekday, they had it to themselves and a few die-hard surfers. They looked like sleek black seals in their wetsuits as they got up on their boards, challenged the waves, fell back in the foaming water and then tried again.

The sky was a bright, bright blue, with the hot sun burning off most of the color. There was no haze or fog to even suggest smog, and gulls wheeled in the windy expanse of sky.

"A loaf of bread," Kevin said suddenly.

"What?"

"We could have fed the gulls."

"Will they come down close to you?"

He turned and stared at her then, the expression in his blue eyes amazed. "Tell me it isn't so. What did you *do* as a kid?"

"I lived in San Francisco."

"Great place for gulls."

"We didn't go to the beach much."

"I guess. Did you ever want to?"

"Yeah."

Kevin laced his fingers with hers, then pulled her back gently so they were both lying on their backs on the beach towels. "I feel like Gregory Peck in *Roman*

Holiday. And you need a nickname, but Princess isn't it. Gillie, the day is yours, until we meet with Mr. Underwood. What did you always want to do at the beach?''

She didn't even hesitate. ''Ice-cream cones.'' Somehow, she knew Kevin wasn't a man who would laugh at her, no matter what she said. He was too kind, too solid, too down-to-earth.

''Ice cream. I knew there was a reason I liked you. The laundry will have to wait, Gillie. Your first day at the beach is much too important.''

AFTER THEIR ICE-CREAM CONES, they rented boogie boards and Kevin took her out into the surf and taught her how to catch waves. Gillian found herself remembering *Jaws*, and when she told him she was worried because she couldn't see the bottom of the ocean, he promptly retaliated by grabbing her foot when she wasn't looking and biting it, then laughing when she screamed.

''I didn't really think it was a shark. It just startled me.''

He merely smiled.

From there, after throwing their wash in the dryer, they took in a movie, an action-adventure film full of nonstop violence and surprises. The audience was composed of mostly boys in their early teens, and Kevin egged the rowdy bunch on, supplying dialogue that wasn't in the film and making Gillian laugh so hard that the usher came down the aisle with his flashlight and asked them to leave.

"You've never been thrown out of a movie before?"

"Never."

"You haven't lived."

After quickly retrieving their laundry, they went back to the hotel and washed up, then dressed and hit the streets again. Kevin rented a scooter, and they went tearing all over town, stopping when they saw an interesting shop or place to pick up something else to eat. It started to rain, and while Gillian's natural impulse was to get in out of the storm, Kevin pulled her out into a grassy park and they ran around in the rain, laughing and getting soaked.

After a quick change, they grabbed a burger, then got out the directions to Alan Underwood's beach house and hit the road.

And this time, as Kevin pulled the Jeep away from the curb, Gillian reached over for his hand without even thinking.

ALAN UNDERWOOD WAS A QUIET MAN, with shaggy dark hair and wire-rimmed glasses. His three cats, Babbage, Turing and Schrodenger, a gray tabby, a black cat and a fluffy gray, were all lined up by the downstairs bathroom door, where the would-be Spike was confined.

"I hated to do it to him," Alan confessed, "but Babbage is pretty territorial, and I didn't want him to get hurt."

"Hold Babbage back and I'll get inside the bathroom," Kevin said.

And Gillian simply stood there, surprised to find herself hoping the cat confined in the bathroom wasn't Spike.

Within seconds, Kevin confirmed her thoughts.

"Nope. But a dead ringer. I would have thought he was Spike myself."

Alan offered them a cold drink, and the three of them ended up on the back balcony, overlooking the small yard.

"Those commercials are great," Alan said, as Turing jumped up on his lap and butted his sleek black head against his arm. "But I've never been able to get these guys to warm up to that catfood. They tried it once and just didn't like it."

"I know what you mean," Gillian said. "I've talked with other cat owners and they've said the same thing."

"And these guys aren't picky eaters."

"Great names," Kevin commented. "Charles Babbage, the British mathematician, right?"

"Right. The first person to build a computer."

Gillian patted her lap. Schrodenger was eyeing her hesitantly, but given encouragement, she jumped up and snuggled into her lap.

Gillian couldn't look at Kevin, her embarrassment was so acute. This man, a stupid jock? She didn't know who Charles Babbage was.

Kevin was clearly enjoying Alan's company. "I read a book about Alan Turing, but I can't remember the name of it. I really liked the part where he broke the Ultra code."

"What's an Ultra code?" Gillian asked.

"The Nazis used it in World War II. Alan Turing was another mathematician," Alan explained. He was, Gillian decided in that instant, a really nice man and not condescending at all.

"And Schrodenger?" she asked.

"A physicist," Alan replied. He gestured toward the small gray cat in Gillian's lap. "My sister Clare found her in a garbage can and gave her away to a woman she knew. Three homes later, Clare said no one really wanted the cat, so I told her to bring her over and she's been here ever since."

"Why didn't anyone want her?"

"She's a little dingy. That's why I named her Schrodenger. I call her the Ding for short."

"What about the cat in the bathroom?" Kevin asked.

Alan's brow furrowed as he ran his large hand over Turing's back. "There's always room for more. Babbage won't be overjoyed at first, but we'll manage."

"What are you going to name him?" Gillian asked.

"Norbert," Alan said quietly. "He looks like a Norbert to me."

"Norbert Weiner, right?"

"Right."

At Gillian's puzzled look, Kevin explained. "Norbert Weiner was the first person who said that the more complex a system is, the more prone it is to break down." He glanced back at Alan. "Good choice. Alan, it's been a pleasure. Thanks for being so concerned about Spike. You've got my number in case any other tabbies should turn up."

"It's on my computer."

As they left, they could hear Babbage, stationed at the bathroom door, growling.

"I KNOW WHERE SPIKE IS," Michael said to his mother.

"Harry, he's lying again."

"Michael, you know what we said would happen if you started lying again."

"But I know where he is! He looks just like the cat on the news—"

"Harry!"

"Michael, stop it! I mean it! You've got to stop this lying, I won't have it! Do you understand me, young man?"

And Michael, staring at his dinner plate, slowly nodded his head.

"YOU'RE SURE I can't just stop home and pick up some—"

"Not where we're going."

"Tell me."

"Okay. We're going to Vegas."

"Vegas! Has Spike been sighted there?"

"This has nothing to do with Spike. This has everything to do with you needing a vacation. Ah, Gillie, it's a dirty job, but someone has to do it."

"Just shut up and drive."

Chapter Six

"Vegas," Kevin told her as the Jeep sped along the desert highway, "is my idea of what hell must be like. A fun hell." His tone was teasing, and she smiled as she glanced at him, then adjusted the sunglasses she'd bought in Huntington Beach against the glare.

They'd started for Las Vegas early the next morning, around six. Alan Underwood had agreed to keep Junior and Big Calico for them until they came back, so now the back seat of the Jeep was empty.

Gillian stretched in her seat, then concentrated on the road. She sometimes felt she was being unfair, making Kevin do all the driving, but he'd assured her he didn't mind.

There was something about being out on the road... It was almost impossible to feel depressed. She didn't have much experience with road trips; most of the vacations she'd taken with her family had been more formal. Plane trips to Switzerland. Christmas in Rome, London, Paris or New York. Wherever her father's business interests had been at the time, that's where the family had found themselves when the holidays had rolled around.

But now . . . everything was so different.

You're feeling the changes. It was impossible not to. With her hair loose around her shoulders, less make-up, and soft, nonrestricting clothing, she felt softer, freer . . . happier. The days they'd spent out in the sun had relaxed her, some of the tension was beginning to leave her body.

And as she stared out at the Nevada desert, she wondered, for the first time in a long time, what she was doing at the Merrill Advertising Agency.

Ben had been good to her; there was no doubt about that. There were even aspects of the work she still found compelling. But as stranger after stranger told her how abysmally bad Kitty Krunchies Kat Food was, she wondered why she was even returning to the fold. She felt tinged with guilt. It had never been her intention to foist an inferior product off on the American public.

"What do you like about Vegas?" she asked over the rush of dry, desert air.

"What's not to like? You've got gambling, plenty of liquor and beautiful women." He grinned at her, then said, "And as I'm traveling with one beautiful woman, who could ask for anything more?"

"Give me a break."

"Look in a mirror. I like the new Gillie. I think she suits you better than the old one. And what the new Gillie needs is a vacation. Tell me when you took the last one."

She hesitated too long to lie, then finally admitted defeat. "I can't remember the last time I was away from the office longer than a weekend."

"I knew it. Well, as hard as it may be for you, you're just going to have to kick back and have a good time."

The tall hotel buildings visible on the horizon were the first indication they were nearing Vegas. Then, as they got closer, they saw the impossibly colorful, sparkling billboards. They looked bright and gaudy, promising fun and excitement in the same way a carnival did.

And Gillian began to fall in love.

They pulled off the highway and drove into town. The heat rushed in on them now that they were moving more slowly, and Gillian could see waves of heat shimmering up off the pavement. Kevin stopped the Jeep at a gas station, and struck up a conversation with the attendant.

"You're going to have a hard time getting a room. I think there are like five conventions in town this weekend." The attendant was a teenager with the brightest red hair Gillian had ever seen. She tried not to stare at the freckles that covered his face and neck.

Kevin flashed her a smile. "Good thing we didn't bring Junior and Big Calico. I don't know if they could have taken the stress of sharing a room with us. Just think, Gillie, we might even be forced to share a room."

"Hah."

"She's not always like this," he confided to the attendant. "It's just that she vacations so rarely."

"Are there any rooms available?" Gillian asked the attendant worriedly.

"Rule number one," replied Kevin smoothly. "If there's a room to be found in this town, I'll find it."

"Just think, Gillie, we might even be forced to share a room," Gillian mimicked as she dropped her bag on the floor by one of the beds in the spacious room.

"C'mon, it's not that bad. Who spends any time in their room in Vegas? There's too much to do."

"Do it without me. I'm taking a nap." She buried her face in the cool, crisp pillow, then let out a sigh of pure relaxation.

"We're getting cranky."

"No, *I'm* getting cranky."

She was drifting off to sleep when she felt him tickling her toes.

"I'm going to kill you."

"I'm going to take a shower, then sleep a little, too. We'll order up some food, then hit the casinos."

"Yes. You're right. Whatever you say. Just let me take a nap."

"Do you want a massage? Your shoulders look kind of tight."

"Just a massage?"

"Gillie, what do you take me for?" His voice sounded wounded. "The type of man who would take advantage of an exhausted female?"

"The type of man who would make me have fun." There was a hint of laughter in her voice.

The massage was wonderful. This was a man who knew his way around the human body. Blissful, relaxed, utterly tension-free, Gillian drifted off to sleep with the sound of the shower running in the background.

When she woke up, the room was dark except for a light coming from the bathroom. She raised her head slowly, breathing in the familiar, clean, bleached-sheets smell of hotel rooms, then glanced over at Kevin's bed.

He was sprawled out beneath the covers, and she couldn't tell if he had any clothes on.

She had to check him out.

What a body. Though it wasn't the first thing she usually noticed in a man—she liked shoulders and eyes—Gillian couldn't remember when she'd been closer to a seminude body that was more beautiful than Kevin's. His skin was smooth and slightly darkened by long hours in the sun. He shifted his arm, and muscles smoothly bunched, then unbunched.

And Gillian watched, fascinated.

She was surprised to find that she loved watching him as much as she wanted, when he couldn't look at her and gauge her response. One-sided intimacy was so easy. She'd liked looking at Bryant, too, until everything that had mushroomed between them had become too painful.

Kevin was truly beautiful, a male animal in his prime and at the height of his powers. Totally fit, healthy and full of life.

Her mind began to wander down more intimate paths, and Gillian closed her eyes and lay her head back down on the pillow.

He'd said he would leave it up to her. If and when the relationship moved into something deeper than friendship. And for the first time since she'd met Kevin MacClaine, Gillian wondered what it would be like to be lying next to him, feeling the warmth of his skin, the touch of those assured hands. He was a gentle man, and there was great strength in that gentleness. She knew with an instinct she was beginning to rely on more and more that he would be a considerate and knowledgeable lover.

And passionate....

He was so passionate about life, how could he separate making love from anything else he did? He'd be capable of great depths of feeling in bed, but he'd also be able to laugh out loud. He had a sheer, animalistic joy in his body, a vibrant energy that transcended any negativity or mundane thinking.

She could feel her face starting to flush, and she opened her eyes and looked at him again.

He made a small sound, something like a moan, and rolled over in the big bed. The sheet dipped low and Gillian's eyes wandered down to his sharply defined abdominal muscles. Never hesitating, her gaze followed the line of dark hair that arrowed its way down his stomach—

She wrenched her attention away from Kevin's body, then got out of bed as silently as possible, not wanting to wake him. He had to be tired after all that driving. Padding over the thick carpeting, she slipped into the bathroom and, after shedding her clothing and turning on the cold spray of water, stepped into the shower.

"WHAT KIND OF A SHOW do you want to see?" Kevin asked. They had decided against room service and now, standing in line at one of Vegas's numerous buffets with plates in hand, they were studying a staggering array of salads.

"Something with dancing." Gillian reached for a chicken-and-pasta salad, but Kevin's next words stilled her fingers on the serving spoon.

"Rule number two. Check out what's at the end of the buffet before committing yourself to the salads at the beginning."

She glanced down the huge buffet and saw a man in in a white apron and cook's cap sharpening his knife. On a large wooden slab table in front of him was a huge roast.

"Oh, that looks really good."

"Pack it in, Sommers. We're going to party tonight and you're going to need the energy."

Once back outside, they walked to one of the many hotels that had a fabulous show, complete with dancing and acrobatics.

"I ate like a pig!"

"I like a woman with an appetite."

Vegas was like a huge carnival, the sidewalks packed with people, the hotels blazing with lights. Even the Golden Arches at the McDonald's on the Strip sparkled, completely made up of glittering lights. The lights were everywhere, blazing oranges, vivid greens and blues, golds and reds.

They still had some time before the show, so they meandered leisurely, people jostling around them. The third time Gillian was pushed away from Kevin by the sea of people, he reached out and took her hand, then put his arm around her.

"I don't think we'd have as good a time if I lost you."

She liked his touch, liked the feel of warm skin and clean shirt next to her cheek when she turned her head. His eyes were dancing with excitement, and she could feel his intense energy transferring itself to her.

Kevin MacClaine was a party in his own right. Vegas was just frosting on the cake.

The show was fabulous. The two free drinks were on the small side, but the dancing more than made up for it. Gillian sat at their tiny table, leaning forward, entranced, soaking up every second. She'd forgotten how much she had missed this, watching people move their bodies, use their muscles to their maximum, thrilling to the grace and beauty of what a dancer could do.

Afterward she couldn't contain her excitement, and Kevin didn't even attempt to bring her down.

"How come you know so much about this stuff? Did you used to dance?"

His question caught her off guard, and she was surprised by the rush of feeling those words engendered.

"Yes. I did."

"I bet you were good."

"Not that good." She couldn't believe her throat was tightening up. Dancing was another dream that had died a long, long time ago. She'd thought she'd forgotten how much it had meant to her, thought the pain would have faded with time. But some things couldn't be dulled, some feelings were destined to stay fresh and intense forever.

"What kind of dancing?"

"I loved it all. Ballet. Modern. Even tap."

"That's why you have such great legs."

"Sexist."

"Honest."

"I used to really love it. I loved going to classes, keeping my body on edge, using all my muscles—"

"Keeping it all on edge. I know what you mean. I still like it, even though some people think it's like being an overgrown jock." When he saw the look on her face, he laughed. "C'mon, all is forgiven. I wouldn't have even said it if I still carried a grudge."

They hit the casinos, Gillian taking three rolls of quarters to the slot machines and walking away with an extra fifty-four dollars. Kevin preferred the blackjack tables, and though she didn't know what was going on, Gillian stayed by his side as he played.

The dealer was amazingly deft, and the excitement around the table was contagious. Words that flew around the table had no meaning for her. Broke, bust, hit, draw, stand, push, stiff, stand pat—the only thing she knew was that Kevin seemed to be winning and was enjoying himself immensely.

He came away with almost five times what she'd won.

"This goes for dinner," he announced, "no-holds-barred. Anything you want. And believe me, whatever you want, you can find it here."

"I think I want a drink."

"Let's go for it."

They settled themselves in comfortable chairs in a cocktail lounge just across from the baccarat room.

"That looks so elegant. Have you ever played it?"

Kevin grinned. "I've heard you have to wear a tux. And as you didn't bring an evening gown, we're out of luck."

Their cocktail waitress was drop-dead gorgeous, with long, blond hair, big blue eyes, an incredible body and dragon-lady fuchsia nails.

Kevin ordered a Rusty Nail and Gillian, deciding that tonight was a night to be daring, said, "I just want one of those drinks with an umbrella in it."

The waitress smiled, her eyes fastened on Kevin, then glided off toward the main bar.

"So, you like Vegas."

"I do. I can't believe it's so close and I've never been here." She met his eyes, suddenly embarrassed by what she wanted to say. "Thanks, Kevin. For bring-ing me along—"

"No problem—"

"For making me have fun."

"Are you having a good time?"

She smiled then, the smile filling her entire body, and nodded her head.

He looked at her for what seemed like a long time, then said "Good" so very softly she almost wasn't sure she heard him say it.

When their drinks arrived, she took a sip of hers. Definitely tropical, and she could taste the rum. She took another sip.

"What's this thing called?" she asked the dragon lady.

"A Zombie."

"An apt description if you have too many of them," Kevin said.

The dragon lady smiled seductively and glided off toward the bar.

"You know," Gillian said, "I've never really been drunk."

"What kind of high school did you go to?"

"Boarding school."

"Didn't they teach you anything there?"

"Just school stuff." She took another long sip of her drink. "This is really good."

"So you never t-ped the front of a rival high school?"

"T-ped?"

"Toilet paper. You never wrapped a rival school in toilet paper?"

"No."

He paused for a second, then asked, "Did you go to a prom?"

"It was an all-girls' school."

"Good God. What a waste."

"But it had an excellent academic reputation," she said, and it suddenly struck her as incredibly funny. She set her drink down and started to giggle.

"I think we'll stop at one of those."

"Now who's being a stuffed shirt?"

"Would you like to get drunk?"

"Is it fun?"

"Not the morning after."

"I'd like to see what it's like. Anyway, I'm not driving, and we're in our own hotel."

"True."

She sighed. "Oh, Kevin, I feel like I have so much I have to catch up on. Do you ever feel like you're really, really different and nobody will ever understand you?"

"All the time."

"Would you take advantage of me?" She took another sip of her drink and eyed him, her green eyes huge in her pale face.

"In a minute."

She laughed then, and when their waitress returned, Kevin ordered another round.

"THIS IS LOADS OF FUN."

"Gillie, don't move around so much. I can't keep my balance if you don't stay still."

"Why is the hallway upside down?"

He started to laugh then. It was kind of funny. Gillian Sommers, advertising executive at the prestigious Merrill Advertising Agency, snockered out of her mind in Las Vegas.

He'd lost her for just a second once they'd left the bar, then found her at the slot machines, carefully putting in the last of the quarters she had in her purse. A dark-haired guy with beefy arms and a jealous wife had tried to pick her up, and Kevin had forestalled a fight by sweeping Gillian up in his arms and starting back toward their room.

Now, as he slid the key into the lock, he knew she would be regretting this little adventure in the morning. After four Zombies, Gillian was going to wake up with one hell of a hangover.

He slid her down on her bed, but she caught his shoulders with her hands and he tumbled down on top of her, breaking his fall with his elbows. The full skirt of her turquoise dress billowed out around them on the bed.

"You *are* having fun with me, aren't you, Kevin?"

Something in that question broke his heart, just a little. "I'm having a lot of fun, Gillie. More fun than I've had in a long time."

"Me too."

There was a short silence as they looked at each other, and he couldn't have quite put into words what changed in her expression, but suddenly he knew she was looking at him in a completely different way.

"We could have even more fun," she said quietly, her eyes never leaving his face.

"Oh, no." He reached up and began to gently disengage her hands from his shoulders.

"Are you attracted to me?" she asked hesitantly, and something in her tone of voice made Kevin stop trying to get free and look down into her face.

"Incredibly."

"Really?"

She was so terribly vulnerable, and it tore at his heart.

"Really. Incredibly. Amazingly. Yes. Yes."

"Then it's okay, because I feel the same way."

Her touch was playing havoc with his senses. He wanted her, but he couldn't take advantage of her. He'd never be able to face himself in the morning, and he couldn't bear the thought of hurting her.

"Gillie?"

She was smiling up at him, lost in her own thoughts, and he couldn't help smiling back down at her.

"Gillie." He kissed her nose. "Gillie, I'm going to undress you and tuck you into bed. All right?"

"Mmm." There was a wealth of meaning in that satisfied sound and he groaned as he untangled himself from her arms. Warm, smooth arms. Feminine arms scented with some sort of perfume she'd bought at Caesar's Palace.

"Sit up now, Gillie. Okay, I'm unzipping—try to stay upright, that's my baby—"

She wasn't wearing a bra, just the skimpiest pair of panties he'd ever seen—and he'd bought them for her. She tried to help him peel off her panty hose, but simply managed to get her fingers all tangled up.

Finally, with Gillian undressed and securely tucked beneath the covers, Kevin sat on the side of the bed and smoothed the coppery waves away from her cheek. Her face was slightly flushed, and she turned her head and kissed his fingers.

"Gillie?"

"Mmm?"

"Can you hear me?"

"Mmm."

"Not here. Not now. Not with you like this. I just couldn't . . . do that to you."

"Okay," she whispered, letting the word out on a soft sigh. "I guess this is fun. I've never been this way before—"

"Shh. Sleep, Gillie." And he smiled ruefully knowing that when she woke she wasn't going to be feeling that terrific. Then, leaning over, he kissed her softly on her forehead.

"You're loads of fun."

"Stuffed shirt?" It was barely a whisper.

"Never."

"Mmm. Good."

She slept. And as he watched the gentle rise and fall of her chest, enjoyed the serene expression on her face, Kevin MacClaine realized he was falling in love.

BIRDY HUMMED AS SHE FILLED the teakettle and set it on the burner. As she reached inside the cupboard for her tea bags, she glanced back and smiled at the tabby tomcat washing his paws. He'd found the one patch of sunlight on the kitchen floor, and was lying in it, enjoying himself.

Sundays were always quiet days. After church she walked home and spent some time in her small garden in front of her apartment. Sometimes Diana called. Or, if Birdy had managed to put a little money aside, she might call her daughter. Then Birdy always attempted to make something a little extra special for dinner. Later in the evening she might phone a friend or two, but it was usually a quiet day, a day of reflection.

She could remember several Sundays in the not too distant past being so lonely. But now, with this cat in her apartment, it seemed much less empty.

Birdy knew she didn't have a clause in her lease that specifically said she could have animals in her small apartment. But that had never stopped her from taking in any of the strays she found.

She watched the tomcat stop washing and stretch out in the sun. He was coming along remarkably well, considering how badly he'd been hurt. She'd babied him mercilessly, feeding him chicken baby food and making up small batches of broth, which he lapped up as quickly as she could make. Now, watching the cat lying contentedly in the sun, she knew it was only a matter of time before his hair would grow back and cover the scar on his leg.

Michael called him "punk cat" because of the way the vet had shaved his leg. She knew this animal had his dignity, and it had been severely bruised. But what surprised her was what an outstanding personality this cat had.

He had swiftly become master of her small apartment, strutting about—if a cat could really strut with a broken leg—as if he owned the place. He was a very affectionate animal, and she sensed great emotion in those gray-green eyes.

She knew he missed someone. The question of his ownership hadn't been a burning one at first because all her energies had been concentrated on making sure he recovered from his ordeal. But now, as she watched the cat, she knew there were times when he looked longingly out the large kitchen window, and she wondered if he thought of home.

Birdy knew she couldn't keep him. It wouldn't be right. He had obviously had a home before she'd found him, people who loved him.

But he made her life just the tiniest bit less lonely, and she wanted to hang on to that feeling, if just for another few days.

The cat's head came up as the teakettle whistled, and Birdy bustled around the small kitchen, shutting off the burner and reaching for a teacup and saucer.

"Just shoot me."

"Gillie, it's not that bad. Drink this."

"Aghhh. What is it?"

"Hair of the dog. A Bloody Mary, easy on the vodka. It'll make you feel better."

She reached for the glass because anything had to make her feel better. Kevin had drawn the curtains and taken the phone off the hook, but she still felt as if the entire chorus of dancers they had seen last night had done a tap dance on her head.

She should have felt stupid. Here she was, at her age, having her first hangover. Doing something that most people did when they were teenagers. Catching up again. She didn't even really know what was behind her impulse to drink enough to lose all vestiges of control.

Yes, you do. The nagging little voice in the back of her mind wouldn't be quieted.

Oh, shut up.

You wanted him to want you and you didn't want to be scared, so you thought this way it might work.

She shut her eyes, wrinkling up her face in self-disgust.

"Gillie? Are you all right?"

She nodded her head, opened her eyes and set the tall collins glass on the bedside table.

"It's not much of a vacation for you, babysitting me."

"I don't mind."

"What were we supposed to do today?"

"That's the whole point of taking a vacation. Things aren't planned out, you kind of play it by ear."

She was silent, considering this and thinking about how much of her life had been ordered, organized and then found wanting.

"What do you feel like doing?" he asked.

"Staying quiet for a while."

"Okay." He sat down on the edge of her bed and Gillian studied him, wondering how one man could manage to look so good in faded blue jeans and a bright turquoise T-shirt with a parrot and the word Tropicana slashed across the front.

"Gillie, I'm going to go down and have breakfast. I won't be gone long. Do you want me to bring you something back up?"

The look she gave him must have been a total reflection of how sick that idea made her because he grinned and, grasping her foot through the blanket, squeezed her toes.

"Guess not. I'll be back soon. You just take it easy."

She watched him leave, surprised to find herself starting to miss him before he was even out the door. Once he shut that same door behind him, she lay back down in the cool confines of her bed and closed her eyes.

You wanted him to want you....

She wondered if it would ever end, that horrible sense of self-doubt that Bryant had planted so carefully. He'd been an expert at seeing where she was weakest, understanding her most secret fears. And he had taken each one out of hiding and used it thoroughly, making her, toward the end of their marriage, think she would never be able to find happiness with anyone, let alone the man she had married.

Gillian sighed as she turned her face into the pillow and closed her eyes. Her head still throbbed, but Kevin had been right and the Bloody Mary had taken that horrible edge off. She wondered at her judgment, drinking so much the night before.

I just wanted not to think so much, not to be afraid. I just wanted it all to happen naturally, the way it does with everyone else but me.

But there was more to it than that. And Gillian, who was beginning to realize she'd been lying to herself for a long time, decided it was past time to come clean.

And if it hadn't worked out, you could have blamed everything on those Zombies. "Oh, it wasn't me, it was those drinks I had." No risk. For what? Just so you wouldn't look stupid.

But you did anyway.

She remembered a little of last night, Kevin carrying her into the room and tucking her in. She'd woken up this morning in nothing but a pair of lace panties, so she knew he'd undressed her. And she had a vague memory of him kissing her forehead, of his fingers stroking her cheek.

You did it so you wouldn't be responsible.

Yet he hadn't taken advantage of her.

She'd wanted him to.

Intimacy was so much less threatening when you were barely conscious.

But it wasn't the right way to start a relationship.

She wondered what it was Kevin saw in her, whether she reminded him of someone in his family or whether it was simply a matter of pheromones. He was endlessly patient with her, even though she'd been less than gracious with him from the beginning of this whole adventure. Gillian squeezed her eyes closed, then bit her lip as she felt the first tear seep through.

She was scared to death because she was afraid she was falling in love with Kevin MacClaine.

She hadn't meant to.

She'd tried her hardest not to.

She didn't want all the pain and heartache love always seemed to entail.

But somewhere along the line, a part of her hadn't listened and she'd started to take that long, sweet dive into total, emotional feeling.

He wasn't what her girlfriends would call a safe man, a warm, roly-poly teddy-bear kind of man. He wasn't the boy next door. He lit her up like the lights along the Vegas Strip, made everything just a little bit brighter, clearer, sharper, funnier. Lovelier.

And so much happier.

She'd never met anyone like him.

My life is a total mess.

She felt as if she were falling apart, and more than anything she wanted to be on top of the world so she could show Kevin that life with her could be a glorious experience, something he would want to explore. She wanted him to know that she wasn't just a dried-up, type-A executive, overworked and joyless and burned out. There had been more life to her at one time, but she'd bottomed out.

She even knew the exact moment she had.

It had seemed so much easier, to stay so busy you didn't have time to see all the ways your life was totally lacking. To keep pushing it all under, denying anything was ever wrong. Ben had tried, once or twice, to get her to talk about it. She'd always rebuffed him. And he'd never been able to get past all her defenses, even though Ben Merrill was one of the smartest men she knew.

The thought slipped into her head and as she stared up at the ceiling, some newly awakened intuition told her that this entire journey had more to it than just finding the Kitty Krunchies Kat Food star.

Maybe Ben is smarter than even I give him credit for.

And then, the next thought.

Did he arrange this whole thing?

She couldn't remember a time in her life when she'd traveled so far, so fast. And not just in physical distance. Was it less than a week ago that they'd been arguing on a rainy road outside Palm Desert? Gillian closed her eyes and remembered even further back, when they had told each other off on the way to the desert.

Something he said . . .

Kevin had been right, his instincts dead on. They never, ever, in a million years would have met and spent time together had it not been for Spike.

And one Kevin MacClaine, whom she had accused of being not too bright and not having too much upstairs, had managed to storm the citadel of her defenses. He'd just blasted right through them, determined to bring her out of her self-imposed deep freeze.

Cajoling.

Teasing.

Caring.

And she was scared to death of him.

Oh, she could handle him, if you counted the superficial way she handled most of the men she knew. But Kevin would want more. He had a different kind of intelligence, something much closer to instinct than logic. He didn't seem to fear emotion the way she did. Probably the result of growing up with all of his sisters.

Had Ben seen it all and decided they were perfect for each other? Would she have time to find out? Because as soon as they found Spike—and she genuinely wanted to find the tabby cat—it was all over.

Maybe he looks at you like a charity case.

She could picture the tabloid headlines.

"Woman who never takes vacation needs to cut loose in Las Vegas."

"Deprived of normal teenage experiences during high school years, stuffed-shirt ad exec goes wild."

She closed her eyes.

Maybe you're simply an amusement to him.

It was more than she could bear.

Sitting up, her head throbbing, she stared at the bathroom door and decided that, somehow, she was going to get inside and take a cold shower, rally and be composed and ready for Kevin when he returned.

Slowly, ever so slowly, she slid off the bed and began to crawl to the bathroom.

The Sunday brunch at the Tropicana Hotel was renowned, even in a town known for its inexpensive and lavish brunches. Kevin sipped his last cup of coffee as he studied the strawberry shortcake he'd built for himself.

There was a piece to the puzzle of Gillian Sommers that was still missing. Even though he knew she didn't perceive herself as particularly beautiful, he knew she couldn't have been out in the world this long without having had some experience with the opposite sex. The law of averages, up against a woman who looked like Gillie, didn't work that way.

And that someone had done something to shut her down.

He took another sip of coffee and wondered what he could do to open her up again without frightening her.

The stuffed-shirt-ad-exec act was just that, an act. More of a defense, really. He'd seen her face at the show the other night, watched her more than he had the dancers. Her expression had been animated, totally lit up. Light-years away from the Gillian Sommers he had first met at that Kitty Krunchies party.

He didn't particularly feel it was his mission in life to insist she have fun, but he wanted her to be happy, and that feeling had a potent magic all its own. And last night he'd realized he was coming to care for her— He grimaced, hating hesitation and qualifications even in his private thoughts.

Hell, he loved her. Head over heels. He didn't know when or how. It had been a physical rush at first, from the moment he'd laid eyes on her at the party. When she'd snubbed him with that frosty look of hers, he'd been enraged. Not normal behavior for him. If a woman truly didn't care for him, his attitude had always been that there was another feminine adventure just around the corner.

Not that he had a casual attitude toward the fair sex. He just really liked women. He couldn't honestly say he'd lived like a monk for the past few years. But he'd never let a woman rattle him the way Gillie had.

When Ben had proposed they hit the road in search of Spike, he'd jumped at the chance. When Gillie had visited the compound, the attraction he'd felt toward her had been just as strong, if not stronger, for having been fueled by a few choice fantasies.

He'd wondered about Ben's proposal, why they both needed to hunt for Spike. Something hadn't seemed quite right. But it had also seemed the perfect chance. After he'd phoned Samantha and made sure his animals would be well taken care of, he'd put all his energies into figuring out the enigma that was Gillie.

And he'd hit a brick wall.

He took another sip of coffee and stared out at the lushly landscaped grounds of the hotel. She'd wanted the liquor to take her out of her head and make her less self-conscious. She'd wanted to make love, but while she was pushing something else away from her. Memories of another man?

He grimaced. He wasn't a man to make love to a woman if there were ghosts in bed with them.

Kevin set the coffee cup down and stared at the rest of his dessert. And he realized it would have tasted a lot better had Gillie been down here with him. Laughing and talking, planning the day ahead of them.

He tasted the shortcake, then pushed the small plate aside and stood up.

There was nothing else to do. He'd tried waiting, being gentle, cajoling her. Trying to make her trust him. Funny thing, he'd had some animals at the compound who reminded him of Gillie. Shy, skittish, afraid to trust. And there came a point in their training, after endless patience and tenderness, when you had to forge ahead or just give up on them and keep them as sheltered pets.

Various plans tumbled through his mind as he walked to the exit of the dining area, then outside into the never-ending world of the casinos. They were always bright and noisy; they never stopped. Most of the hotels were so self-contained you had no idea whether it was day or night; you could lose all sense of time.

He had just about exhausted all his plans for Gillie when he saw the display in the gift store.

Just the thing.

Smiling to himself, the beginnings of a plan unfolding in his mind, he went inside.

SHE WAS DRYING HER HAIR when she heard the key in the lock. Already dressed in shorts and a tank top, Gillie remained on the bed as Kevin walked into their room, a bag from the hotel's gift shop in his hand.

''Feeling better?''

She nodded her head determinedly.

"Great. I saw this and thought of you. If you put it on now, we can go outside and catch some sun."

He threw the bag on her bed, the gesture deceptively casual. And Gillie restrained herself from tearing it open, scattering tissue paper everywhere.

Instead, she opened it slowly, savoring the thought that Kevin had wanted to bring her a present.

When she saw what it was, she started to smile.

"I think this is a present for you, not for me."

The tiniest jade-green bikini tumbled out of the bag. As Gillian held it up and checked the size, she remembered that, of course, Kevin would have known what size to buy. He'd bought her clothing before.

"I can't lie to you, Gillie. I thought about what you'd look like in it."

"Yeah?"

"You may be an inactive slug, but you still have a dancer's body."

Her chin lifted just a fraction. "I still do some of the stretching exercises, when I think about it."

"Go throw it on, then pull what you have on over it. I'll get dressed out here and we'll hit the pool."

THE TROPICANA HAD TRULY BEEN an inspired choice. Aside from having the largest swimming pool in the world, the hotel boasted a water slide and three Jacuzzis. One end of the pool even had a swim-up blackjack table, complete with a money drier.

Gillian was still unfastening her shorts by the time Kevin had undressed down to his bathing suit. She watched as he walked over to the diving board and dove into the turquoise water.

She met him beneath the man-made waterfall and was slightly startled when he swam straight up to her and put his arms around her.

"I couldn't think of a better way to get most of your clothes off," he whispered, a wicked gleam in his eyes. Then he looked at her for a long moment, bent his head and kissed her.

The warmth of his mouth was a complete contrast to the coolness of the water. Gillian felt herself become completely pliant in his arms and was almost afraid of sinking into the water until she realized he was keeping them both afloat.

It was a quick kiss, a public kiss, but a kiss that made his eventual intentions completely clear. Her hands fluttered nervously for just an instant, then she felt the smooth skin of his shoulders. Her hand slid up the back of his neck, her fingers tangled into his wet hair.

When he broke the kiss, the expression in his blue eyes was playful, yet she had the strangest sense he was watching her closely.

"Okay?" he asked softly.

She nodded her head.

"I thought we could go out to dinner tonight. Anything you want."

Gillian looked up at him, her eyes narrowed against the spray coming off the waterfall.

"Something exotic."

"I'll think of something."

"Don't let me drink anything."

He laughed.

"And I want to do some shopping before we go out. The blue dress is a little worse for wear."

"Deal." The expression in his face went from playful to serious in a heartbeat. "I want you to know, Gillie, that tonight you're in charge. Nothing's going to happen unless you give the go-ahead."

His sensitivity touched her, and she felt her eyes start to fill. How did this man know she was so scared to start all over again? How did he seem to know how badly she'd been hurt?

"Hey, I didn't mean to start you crying." Now he was all concern.

"It's okay. It's more than okay." She leaned into him, her arms sliding around his neck, his body warm against hers.

"It's wonderful."

Chapter Seven

A quick trip to The Fashion Show, the largest mall in Las Vegas, outfitted Gillian for the night ahead. And in Las Vegas, even malls were different. This one had valet parking, and a Promenade of Stars—a walkway with the Star's handprints and signatures immortalized in cement.

Gillian had wondered if Kevin would be up to a typical shopping trip with her, but he proved he had patience and endurance as she searched for the perfect dress. They looked at Bullock's, Neiman-Marcus, JAG, Courreges and Cache before she found the perfect little black dress at Saks.

"Sorry it took so long," she admitted. They'd stopped at Häagen-Dazs for a quick ice-cream cone, and now all she had to do was buy a pair of shoes.

"I'm just glad you're doing the shopping this time. I wouldn't have known what to get you."

She just smiled. He hadn't seen the dress on her, and it was simply beautiful. Tight, short and drop-dead sexy. She'd started shopping with one thing in mind, and that was to have Kevin see her in a completely different light tonight.

After shoes, she couldn't resist the endless counters of makeup, and she browsed while Kevin checked out a bookstore. Then, packages in hand, they returned to their room at the Tropicana.

"CAN WE GO DANCING TONIGHT?" she called through the bathroom door.

"Anything you want. It's your evening."

Gillian returned her attention to the mirror, glad she'd succumbed to temptation and bought out the makeup counter at Bullock's. She loved getting dressed up, and as she'd put on her face she'd realized she couldn't remember the last time an evening out had excited her more.

The face that looked back at her was the same one she saw in the mirror every morning—but happier and much more dramatic. She'd shadowed her eyes with coppers and browns, even a little gold highlight. Her hair, left loose for so long, seemed to take on a life of its own. She'd tamed it with two combs, twisting it back off her face but still letting it fall free the way Kevin liked it. She'd gone wild with mousse and spray and gel, and the effect was a lion's mane of copper-colored waves.

And the dress . . . Black, with a modest front, incredibly low-cut back and short skirt. She'd remembered that Kevin liked her legs, so she'd bought black, impossibly high heels. A rhinestone pin and earrings, bought at the jewelry counter near makeup, completed the outfit.

But she still had to put everything on. Now, staring at her reflection in the large bathroom mirror, clad only in the black satin-and-lace underwear she'd bought while Kevin had thought she was still looking at makeup, Gillian thought of the evening ahead.

You're in control. Didn't Kevin say so? Nothing's going to happen unless you give the go-ahead.

The funny thing was, she wanted everything to happen. She felt as if she had champagne in her blood, making her feel light and free. As if a huge weight had been lifted off her.

She shut her eyes as her thoughts continued, drawing her deep inside herself. Gillian took a deep breath, trying to slow her rapidly beating heart.

Step-by-step. Just take it step-by-step.

Bryant had scarred her in some ways. But she knew things would be different with Kevin.

If you want it to happen.... If you let it happen....

The sharp rap on the door jarred her out of her thoughts.

"Hey! Let's get going, Gillie."

She opened her eyes, then almost laughed out loud when she saw she'd unconsciously crossed her fingers. As she took the dress off the hanger and started to wriggle into it, she wondered what Kevin's reaction was going to be.

HE DIDN'T disappoint her.

"Gillie." It was all he seemed capable of saying as he stared at her.

"Did I look that bad before?" she teased.

"No, not at—God, Gillie, that's some dress."

She took a deep breath. "I bought it for you."

Something in his eyes changed, and she was so glad she'd told him.

"You look gorgeous."

"So do you." She didn't know where he'd fit a suit into the small bag he carried, but he looked wonderful. As the sudden thought struck, she couldn't resist laughing out loud.

"What?"

"Is this what a prom is like?"

"Better. Much better." Again, that mischievous gleam she loved came into his eyes. "I don't have to take you home tonight. Dad isn't watching the clock. The night's still young."

She walked to his side and curled her hand around his arm. She felt the strength in those muscles and knew this man would never, ever hurt her.

"Let's go."

THEY ATE DINNER at Arabian Nights. She'd wanted something exotic and Kevin had found it for her. They entered the restaurant through a tiny store that offered everything from canned goods to beautifully inlaid backgammon sets. Once in the doorway of the actual restaurant, the scent of exotic spices assailed them, and Gillian gave herself over to the fantasy.

And what a fantasy it was. They sat in a small dimly lit room with low brass tables, red padded benches and plenty of soft cushions. The walls were covered with striped, colorful fabrics, and a belly dancer moved sinuously from table to table.

Gillian discovered Kevin was an adventurous diner, the same as she was, and she wondered at what he'd pretended to be earlier when she'd told him how she liked sushi. They shared an assortment of salads, cucumber, *hummus* and *baba ghanouj*, then moved on to lamb shish kebab and grilled chicken with spices.

"When you ask for exotic, you get exotic," he teased her. They were finishing their meal with baklava and Arabic coffee with just a touch of cardamom, served in a Bedouin coffeepot. "Now, what else do you want to do?"

They went to a magic show and watched the master magician make an elephant disappear and a Bengal tiger float in space. Kevin was particularly impressed with the latter, as he had watched Samantha work with big cats several times.

"What now?" Gillian asked when she and Kevin were back out on the Strip again.

"The lady wants to dance, she gets to dance."

Kevin's choice was perfect, Cleopatra's Barge in Caesars Palace. They laughed themselves sick as they rode the moving sidewalks into the massive hotel, while booming commentary told them about how ruthless and extravagant Caesar was. Cleopatra's Barge, the only dance floor on a floating barge, was easy to find off one of the large corridors. The band was excellent, rock-and-roll with a beat, and Kevin was a good dancer. Gillian found herself either dancing or laughing or both as she took in ostrich feather fans, statues of ancient pharaohs, furled sails and the cocktail waitresses clad in minitogas.

Kevin raised an eyebrow when Gillian ordered a Coke, but she merely smiled.

They walked through the hotel after Cleopatra's closed. Kevin brought her a Caesar Bear, a stuffed bear in a toga with a crown of laurel leaves. They had coffee and cake at Cafe Roma, then walked back out into the cool, desert night.

"Back to the room?" he asked.

She was holding his hand, and her fingers tightened slightly as she nodded her head.

They walked down the Strip for a bit, enjoying the blaze of riotous color, the coolness of the night air, and watching all the different people who congregated in Las Vegas.

But they weren't even past the Barbary Coast when Gillian's shoes began to pinch her feet.

"I'm sorry, it's just that they're new. I think my feet have swollen up a little—"

"No problem."

She let out something that vaguely resembled a squeak as he swept her up into his arms.

"You don't have to do this—"

"Think of it this way, Gillie. If I wore heels and they were hurting my feet, you could carry me."

The image was so outrageous she started to laugh. She didn't even feel the slightest bit self-conscious. People around them were smiling, and Gillian simply put her arms around Kevin's neck and let him walk down the Strip, carrying her.

He didn't even seem winded, even when he set her down by the Jeep. They'd parked in the lot behind the Vagabond Inn then walked up to the Strip, as the Tropicana was at the far end of town and not within walking distance.

"Any other fun thing you'd like to do?" he asked.

"What time is it?"

"Five twenty-three."

She hitched her Caesar Bear up higher beneath her arm. "Let's go back to the room."

He was quiet as he drove, and she wondered what he was thinking the entire way. When Kevin finally opened the door to their hotel room, she stepped inside and walked quickly into the bathroom.

Once inside, she leaned against the sink and thought about the direction what was left of the night could take.

One thing was certain, she couldn't spend the rest of the night in this bathroom.

She stepped outside. Kevin had taken off his suit jacket and was standing at the window, looking down over the sprawl of colorful lights that made up the city. He turned toward her as she came into the room, and for a moment they just looked at each other.

Kevin finally broke the silence.

"I meant what I said, Gillie. You're in control. Nothing is going to happen tonight unless you want it to. I'll sleep in my bed, I'll sleep in yours, I'll spend the rest of the night out in the casino if that's what you want."

She swallowed against her suddenly dry throat. "What do you want?"

"I want you. You know that. But I don't want you to be scared or have any hesitations about being with me. I wouldn't get any pleasure at all out of seeing you scared."

She looked down at the carpet. "Is it that obvious?"

"What."

"That I'm scared."

"Gillie." There was such concern in his voice. He came toward her slowly, then wrapped his arms around her. She could feel his heart beating, her cheek against his chest.

"Not scared," he said softly. "Maybe...hesitant. I think you're a woman who gives over a lot when she loves. And I want you to feel it's right, not something you had to do to make me happy."

She nodded her head.

"Tell me what you want."

Tell me what you want. It was an awesome responsibility, having it all in her hands. Yet she knew what Kevin was doing, knew the final responsibility had to be hers.

"I want...to be with you. But—"

"But," he prompted gently.

"But I'm scared," she whispered.

"What scares you?" His hand was warm on her bare back, caressing her skin.

"That I won't... That I can't..." She swallowed again, then forced the next words out. "You're the first man I've thought of being with...this way...since my husband."

His hand stilled, then he said, "You're divorced?"

She nodded her head.

"Me, too."

She stepped away slightly, looked up at him. Still the same Kevin of the warm blue eyes and steady smile.

"What happened?"

"She decided she wanted a different type of life-style than the one I could provide for her."

He made it sound so cut and dried, but she knew the pain behind divorce, and so she slowly nodded her head.

"It must have hurt you."

He touched her cheek. "By the time Jeane and I got to talking about a divorce, the marriage had been over for a long time."

"I know what you mean." Gillian broke away from him gently, then walked over to her bed and sat down. She didn't look at him as she took off her heels and began to rub her feet.

She sensed rather than saw when Kevin walked over to his bed and sat down, facing her.

"Do you want to talk about it?"

She thought of Bryant, of all they had been through together, and she knew Kevin couldn't possibly know what was going on inside her until he knew what had come before.

She nodded her head.

"Would you like some wine? It might help relax you."

She hadn't realized how tightly she was holding her body until he mentioned it.

"Yes." Her tone was grateful, and she realized she was reaching for anything he could offer her, any-thing to make things easier.

He ordered wine, and she went in the bathroom and took off her dress, took down her hair and wrapped herself in the emerald silk robe.

When she came back out of the bathroom, she noticed he'd changed into a pair of jeans. They talked of inconsequential things until the wine arrived, then she took her glass and walked over to the large window overlooking Las Vegas. She could see the Strip, the colored lights blazing brilliantly against the night sky. Soon it would be sunrise, and she suspected even then this city wouldn't sleep.

She took a sip of wine, then walked over to the lamp and turned it off. The room was in darkness as she walked slowly back toward the window and stared outside.

"Tell me about it," Kevin said, his voice breaking the silence.

She took another sip of wine to steady herself, then began to force the words out. She hadn't talked about Bryant in a long time, and she still didn't like to. But she couldn't come to Kevin with anything standing between them.

"I met him through my father. He'd bought a baseball team, and Bryant was their pitcher. He was...everything I always thought I'd wanted in a man. I was never very comfortable around men. Even though I grew up with three brothers, I was always away at school. Especially after my mother died.

"Maybe I married him because I wanted to get out of the house. Maybe because he was the first man who had really seemed to pay attention to me. My father wasn't a bad father, he was just...cold."

"How old were you when you married him?"

"Nineteen. I was barely out of school. My father gave us a house in San Francisco, Bryant continued playing for the team and I went to school. The first few years were all right, except—"

She took another sip of wine. Remembering hurt far more than she would have thought it would. It seemed like all of it had happened so long ago, but talking about it again, facing those feelings, brought all the emotion rushing back to the surface.

"It was like the romance and courtship was just on the surface and marriage was the goal. Just like a home run. Once we were married, the romance died. And we never did get the sex thing right."

She swallowed against the sudden tightness in her throat. There. It was out. Maybe he wouldn't even want to be with her once he knew she'd failed in the most intimate way possible.

"What happened?"

This was harder than she'd ever imagined it would be, and Gillian suddenly realized she'd never told anyone. She'd never had any reason to tell anyone. Not her father, certainly. They'd never been that close, and he would have been horrified had she instigated such a conversation. And to everyone else, she'd been Gillian Sommers, carefree daughter of one of San Francisco's richest men.

"We fought a lot, and one time he told me he'd never been really happy with me. I mean, in bed. He said—he said he'd had a lot of experience before marrying me and that I didn't . . . score that high, that I didn't know what to do—" The lights were blurring in front of her eyes and she blinked quickly, rapidly, hating the way the emotion was making her voice tighten and climb just a little higher.

"You were a virgin when you married him." Kevin said it quietly, absolutely no emotion in his voice.

She leaned her forehead against the glass, grateful for the coolness. "I thought— I was happy there hadn't been anyone else. I loved Bryant and I wanted to give him so much—" She stopped as a sob rose up in her throat, then she swallowed it down.

"Was that why you divorced?"

"No. It was—he went on the road a lot, with spring training and all the games. I used to go with him in the beginning. I tried to schedule my classes around his traveling. I liked some of the men on the team, they were great guys. But then he stopped asking me along, so I decided I'd just try harder.

"I kept myself busy while he was away, I took more classes. I learned to cook, I tried to improve myself. I kept thinking there had to be something else I could do to make him happier with me."

"Why did you divorce him?"

"I was unpacking his suitcase and I found a pair of panties. Black lace. They weren't my size. I asked him about them and he said he had—he had these needs, and as he wasn't getting them satisfied at home, he'd— He said it was a one-night stand, and he told me it wouldn't happen again."

"But it did."

She took another sip of her wine, then set the glass down on the table by the window.

"Again and again. I think in the end I knew he wanted to hurt me. He had one girlfriend who even traveled on the team jet. She used to phone the house in San Francisco and if I answered, she'd hang up."

"The bastard."

"But if I had been—"

"*Don't.* Don't make excuses for him."

She was silent, wondering what Kevin thought of her. Wondering if he was starting to regret the fact that they'd been thrown together because of a missing cat.

Gillian couldn't even see the lights distinctly now, they were blurring as she remembered. "My father told me I was crazy. He kept telling me what a brilliant future Bryant had, how any woman would be overjoyed to be married to him. When I told him Bryant was unfaithful, he told me to be practical."

She could feel Kevin's silence.

"But I couldn't. It hurt too much. I divorced him. It was the first divorce in our family and my father was enraged. I can remember sitting in my room in his house and wondering how he could be the way he was and make a divorce more important than his own daughter."

"What happened?"

"I left. I couldn't stay there anymore. I packed up a couple of bags, closed down my bank account and headed for Los Angeles. I didn't talk to my father for almost a year, but in that time I started to really grow up. I wasn't destitute, I had a small trust fund from my grandmother. And I had an excellent education.

"I decided I wanted to go into advertising, and I managed to get a job at the Merrill Agency after I'd worked at a few others. Ben was my mentor, and you know the rest."

The sun was just starting to come up behind the mountains as she turned away from the window.

"I don't want to talk about it anymore, okay?"

"Okay. I'm sorry he hurt you, Gillie."

"It wasn't your fault."

"I can still be sorry."

"Okay."

She walked over to her bed on unsteady legs, then lay down and took a couple of deep breaths. It was several minutes before she heard Kevin's voice.

"You know, as equal as men and women are supposed to be, I still believe that one of the main places a man protects a woman is in bed. And I'm not talking about birth control."

She opened her eyes and turned toward him. He was lying on his bed, staring at the ceiling.

"He was a wimp, Gillie. A wimp and a coward. I would have respected him more if he'd told you it wasn't there for him anymore, the feelings had died. But to put it all on you..." He let the sentence trail off.

She was silent for a few seconds, then blurted out, "I've never told anyone before. Not the whole truth. I told my father Bryant had been unfaithful, but I never told anyone what he said about me. I just thought you should know what you're getting into."

Now he turned his head and met her eyes, and the expression on his face could only be called intense.

"*That's* why you told me? Because you really don't believe you have it in you to make a guy happy? Gillie, he was emotionally *abusing* you, telling you that! What kind of a man was he, telling you you couldn't turn him on and then running around on you?" As quickly as he asked the question, Kevin seemed to find the answer. "He was justifying himself, Gillie. He was trying to get you to believe it was all your fault, and he was full of it.''

She reached across the small space separating their beds, found his hand and clung to it.

''But it—it never really happened for me.'' She couldn't meet his eyes, telling him something so intimate, so she looked away. ''I never felt anything. Not what you're supposed to feel.''

''Not with him you didn't.''

She couldn't meet his eyes.

She couldn't not meet them.

And she found total, quiet determination.

''Could you—'' She stopped and cleared her throat, then looked away. ''You told me that I was in charge—''

''Whatever you want, Gillie.''

''Could we just kind of sleep together? I mean, in one bed? And not do anything yet? I don't know if I'm up to anything right now, but I'd like to be close.''

In answer, he got up off his bed and with one lithe movement, lay down beside her.

''Okay?''

She nodded her head.

''Can I put my arms around you—''

''Yes.''

''Just like this, just snuggling up—''

When her cheek finally came to rest against his bare chest, she let out a long breath, some of the tension leaving her body.

''You're so warm.''

''I'm a warm kind of guy.'' There was a smile in his voice.

She ran her hand lightly over the hair on his chest.

"You're kind of hairy."

"It's good in my line of work. Makes the animals trust me more."

When she started to laugh, she knew everything was going to be all right.

"It's Spike, Birdy, I *know* it is."

"Michael, there are a lot of tabby cats in Los Angeles. We don't know for sure." But Birdy was hedging and she knew it.

"I told Mom, and she told Dad to tell me to stop lying. But it's *him*, I know it is. He looks just like the cat in the commercial! And there's a *reward* out for him, so we could take Spike in and get all sorts of money."

She looked down at him. Michael was a little more eager to get the reward than to actually do the right thing, but Birdy knew his heart was usually in the right place.

"Bring me the poster with the picture and phone number on it. If I think it's Spike, we'll phone his owner."

"All right!"

Once Michael left, Birdy finished her tea, then walked slowly back to her bedroom. The large tabby was stretched out on top of her afghan, in the one patch of sun. He was coming along splendidly; his recuperative powers were amazing.

She didn't need the picture. She'd simply wanted to keep this big cat just a little longer. Funny how an animal with such an outstanding personality could make a home so much less lonely.

If Michael had been thinking, he would have realized there was no need for him to go home and bring a poster back tomorrow.

She wet her lips, then softly called to the cat.

"Spike."

The large head came up, the expressive green-gold eyes focused alertly on her face. Then he meowed.

"Spike." She sat down next to him on the double bed, then scratched him beneath his chin.

"So you really are Spike."

A rumbling purr was her only answer.

"And do you know everyone is out looking for you?"

He butted the top of his head against her hand.

"I'm sure they miss you." She paused for a second, then said, "I'm sure I'll miss you when you're gone, Spike."

The green-gold eyes were steady as he began to lick her hand.

THE PAIN WOKE HER UP.

For a moment she didn't remember where she was. The room was dark, but the smell reminded her she was in a hotel room. The warm, muscular arm wrapped firmly around her reminded her she was in bed with Kevin MacClaine.

He must have pulled the curtains shut, she thought, then braced herself for another wave of pain.

She tensed against it, every so slightly, trying not to move on the big bed. But she knew as soon as she moved that he was awake.

"Gillie?" His voice was gravelly, full of sleep.

She took a breath, then caught it as the pain took hold again.

"Are you all right?" he asked softly. The pressure from his arm had changed. He'd been holding her tightly against the warmth of his body, but now his touch was concerned. Gentle.

"Stomach—" It was all she could manage to get out.

"I'm calling a doctor." He started to get out of bed.

"No— Bag. My bag."

He understood, and within seconds the bag containing all her over-the-counter medication was within reach. Kevin uncapped the Pepto Bismol and held it to her lips.

She swallowed some, but it almost came back up.

"Sick—"

He helped her into the bathroom. Sometime during the night she'd taken off the silk robe, and now, clad only in bikini panties and a low-cut bra, her hair a tangled mess and the makeup she'd so carefully applied slightly smeared, she felt like a complete and utter failure.

"Sorry—"

Then an amazing thing happened, an utterly amazing and perfect thing. Kevin sat down on the bathroom floor, gently pulled her into his arms and began to rock her.

And she clung to him, her fingers digging into his shoulders, her stomach burning with pain, and she began to cry.

"Failure—"

"Don't talk, Gillie."

"I feel like such a failure."

"No. Never."

"Kevin." She clung tighter.

"Don't try to talk."

She cried and cried, more from the release than the pain, and all the time she could feel the strength in his arms, the steady beating of his heart. And she wondered at this man's capacity to love, even after he'd probably been hurt as much as she had.

When she couldn't cry anymore, she tried to make him understand how she felt.

"I'm going to let you down," she whispered. Her head felt swollen and sore, her nose stuffed up.

"No. You could never do that."

He rocked her a little more in silence, then said softly, "Gillie, just tell me what you want."

"I want you to make it all better." She started to cry again, and he held her tighter.

"It's okay."

"I think I'm going crazy."

"I know, baby."

"You make me crazy."

She felt his smile. "I hope so. Tell me what else you want. I'll make sure you get it."

And she knew at that moment, with the most incredible sense of total peace, that she could ask for anything and that was part of what love was.

"I just— I want you to hold me close."

"I won't let you go."

He rocked her until the pain subsided, then carried her to bed and tucked her in. She reached for his hand and he understood what she wanted and climbed into the big bed with her and held her until she fell asleep.

THE NOISE. BIRDY COULDN'T DRIFT off to sleep because of the noise. It sounded like a baby's wail, and for a minute she thought she was a young mother and Diana was crying, demanding to be held or changed or fed.

The noise was getting louder now, like a siren. She opened her eyes, totally disoriented, and found Spike on her chest, meowing and batting at her face.

Birdy had been tired when she'd gone to sleep, and now she wanted nothing more than to continue sleeping. But Spike's large paw caught her cheek roughly, and she struggled back to consciousness.

Something smelled.

Smoke.

She opened her eyes and forced herself to sit up, swinging her legs over the side of her double bed and wincing as she realized one had fallen asleep. Ignoring the pinpricking sensation, she scooped Spike up in her arms and headed out into her living room.

The kitchen.

A haze of gray smoke filled her living room, and Birdy grasped Spike tightly with one arm as she pushed her loose hair out of her eyes. Once inside her small kitchen, she saw the gas burner blazing merrily away beneath her teakettle. The water had long ago evaporated, and now the kettle was burning.

Setting Spike down on the kitchen table, she reached over and quickly turned off the burner, then took a pot holder and moved the kettle off the hot burner. It was only afterward, when she'd opened her kitchen windows and front door, leaving the screen door locked, that she sat down in the overstuffed chair in her living room and began to shake.

Spike hobbled into the living room, wound clumsily around her feet and meowed up at her.

Fiercely, with all the love she possessed in her small wiry frame, Birdy scooped the tabby cat up into her lap and pressed her cheek against the top of his head. Tears gathered in her eyes and ran down her wrinkled cheeks.

Oh, you wonderful, wonderful cat.

She sat with Spike for a long time, watching the tendrils of smoke fade away into the still night air. She'd neglected to get the batteries replaced on her smoke alarm because she'd been afraid of falling when she installed them. Her landlord, Mr. Russell, a rather cantankerous sort of man, didn't like the older people living in his building because there wasn't much profit to be made. They'd lived there so long their rents were extremely low. Birdy was careful never to ask her landlord for anything. She didn't want to call attention to herself.

Just last month, Emily in the back unit had been moved to a nursing home. That was Birdy's ultimate nightmare. And if Mr. Russell even suspected she'd almost burned down his building, he'd make sure she was shipped off to her daughter's.

She already knew Diana would not want her around.

After a while, she shut the living room door, then went back into her kitchen, Spike trailing her. She opened a can of tuna and put it on one of her favorite china plates, then set it down on the floor and petted the cat while he made short work of it. Then Birdy took out a small saucepan and boiled some water. She carefully shut the burner off and took the pan off the stove, then fixed herself a much-needed cup of tea.

Spike was finishing up his tuna when her tea had cooled enough for her to sip it. He sat at her feet while he clumsily washed himself.

"Oh, Spike, what am I going to do?" Birdy asked the cat. "I don't want to give you up, but I know it's not right to keep you. I know you have people who miss you." She reached down and stroked behind his ears. And realized he had probably, one way or another, saved her life.

Guardian angels come in many guises.

Gazing straight in front of her and seeing nothing, Birdy sent up a silent thanks that a street-smart, rough-and-tumble tabby had been sent her way.

SHE COULDN'T STOP LOOKING at him when she woke up.

Even exhausted, he was beautiful.

And Gillian, feeling a sense of calm and certainty that was rare for her, snuggled closer to him, knowing she had made the right decision.

She was curled closely around him when his eyes slowly opened. And she knew his body had responded before his brain was fully functional, because she could feel those changes, pressed as close to him as she was.

She'd come awake once she'd slept for a few hours, her eyes flying open, and she'd realized Kevin was a man like no other she'd ever met. Smart, funny, sexy. But more than that—open, direct and compassionate. In the short time she'd known him, he'd shown her more kindness and compassion than almost anyone else except Ben.

After Bryant, her sexual feelings had been shut down for a long time. She'd heard from some of the women in her office about the sexual binges they'd gone on after their divorces had come through. And she'd wondered at herself, at what was wrong with her that she should have absolutely no desire.

Now this intense feeling she had for Kevin—it was certainly stronger than what she'd felt for Bryant, and she'd been married to the man for eight years.

Kevin was awake now and looking down at her, his eyes questioning.

"I'm ready," she said.

"Now?"

"Uh-huh."

"Your stomach—"

"Is fine." She touched his chest, amazed that one man could generate such heat.

"You're sure?"

She melted completely when she realized he was still worried about her, this wonderful, wonderful man.

Feeling happiness well up inside her, she snuggled even closer, then slid up the sheets until her lips were against his ear.

"You men," she whispered. "You're all alike. My life is caving in and you take me out on the town, feed me exotic food, take me dancing, talk me into a few glasses of wine—"

He was laughing now.

"—listen to all my problems, spend the entire night getting me through stomach pains, and *boom*, we're in bed together."

"I suppose we could wait a few more minutes." But his hand was already at her back, deftly unsnapping her black bra.

She bit his ear lobe. "You know, in a crazy way I still hate you."

"I know." He was cupping her breast, and she couldn't remember anything ever feeling as good.

"You have freckles," she whispered as he kissed her neck. "I don't even like freck—ahh, freckles."

"Mmm." Now he was kissing her neck, behind her ear, while his hand was still on her breast, gently pinching the nipple.

"You're not even my type. This is never—ohh—*never* going to work. I don't like blond hair on men—"

"Neither do I—"

Then he was kissing her and she couldn't think of anything else to say.

Chapter Eight

When she finally woke up, she couldn't stop looking at Kevin and marveling at this man who had given her so much.

Kevin had exorcised Bryant's judgment of her forever.

He was still asleep, one arm thrown up over his eyes, the other across his chest. Though they'd remained snuggled up against each other throughout most of the night, when she'd finally opened her eyes there had been just enough space between them so she didn't disturb him.

And Gillian, her head turned so she could look at him all she wanted, had never felt better in her entire life.

I still believe that one of the main places a man protects a woman is in bed.

When realization finally hit, it was all so simple.

Bryant had been a boy.

Kevin was a man.

A man who had led her through lovemaking and made sure she experienced incredible pleasure. A man who never rushed her or made her feel quietly inadequate, simply let her find her own pace. A man who had caused her body to blossom beneath his expert touch and whispered words.

She'd never believed it could all be so pleasurable. Gillian had never truly understood what drove both men and women to express their sexuality. But now she did. This man, lying beside her, had given her so much more than an extended vacation. He'd done so much more than simply show her the destructiveness of her present course through life.

He'd helped her find and reclaim her sensuality, her sexuality, her sense of trust in herself.

I gave up hope of ever falling in love. Then he found me and taught me how.

There was such a difference between her ex-husband and Kevin. And as they were the only two men she'd ever been intimate with, she couldn't help comparing them. Both had the bodies of athletes, strong, muscular and sure. But Bryant had seemed to block himself off from her, while Kevin had urged her closer and closer until it had truly felt like they'd slipped inside each other's skins.

And the aftermath... There had always been that horrible sense of incompletion with Bryant. It wasn't as if she'd been truly ignorant about her body when she'd told Kevin she'd never found fulfillment. She'd just never found it in her marital bed, with her ex-husband.

She smiled and could feel her face growing warm as she remembered the intense feelings she'd had in Kevin's arms. Gillian closed her eyes as the blush deepened. The first time she'd reached fulfillment, she'd thought they were done. Kevin hadn't laughed at her innocence, but had simply assured her they were far from finished.

Pleasure had peaked within her until she'd lost count of how many times it happened. And as Kevin continued to make love to her, she'd realized there had been a subtle undercurrent in her relationship with Bryant. He had never truly liked women. There were certain things her ex had considered off limits sexually, and she realized Bryant was not totally at ease with women's bodies.

Where Bryant had had their sex life rigidly choreographed, Kevin had been spontaneous, giving, totally at ease with his body and hers. The feelings she had felt, the sensations that had flared through her, the ecstasy that had been almost painful and at one point had caused her to cry, all seemed light-years away from her marital relationship.

And to think I could have died and never known this even existed....

The total realization of what was truly possible between two people when they were willing to be vulnerable, when the feeling between them was so strong, overwhelmed her.

She was feeling sleepy again and decided not to fight it. Gillian slid across the short distance and curled up next to Kevin. His skin was so warm, and even in sleep he moved his arm to encircle her.

Totally content, she drifted off to sleep securely in his arms.

WHEN SHE WOKE UP, he was watching her.

"What time is it?"

"Does it matter?"

She smiled then, and he leaned over and kissed her.

"How do you feel?"

"Wonderful." She closed her eyes, then rubbed her cheek against her pillow. "But why am I still so tired?"

She felt him move against her, slide his arms around her. "You were letting down a lot of emotional walls. It wasn't just the sex."

She opened one eye. He was grinning.

"Not that I'm complaining about the sex."

"Hmm." She stretched, a sinuous, catlike stretch. "I was all right, wasn't I?"

"The words 'all right' don't even begin to describe it."

She laughed then, and he caught the laugh with a quick kiss. Her hands caught his shoulders, then slid up into his hair. It was all there in a heartbeat, she wanted him again, wanted the closeness and the passion. It had never been this way with any other man, and even though the intensity of it frightened her just a little, she wanted to feel it all over again.

"I thought," Kevin whispered, "we might spend the day in bed, order up some food, discuss the great books—"

"Mmm-hmm." She looked up at him, feeling younger and freer than she had in years. "Whatever you want."

"Only if you agree."

"I do."

"How's your stomach?"

"Hungry."

"And the rest of you?"

"Fine."

"I didn't hurt you?"

"No."

"I thought I might have gotten a little carried away at the end. I know you haven't been with anyone for a long time."

"Kiss me."

He did, then whispered, "I've created a monster."

THEY ORDERED EVERY APPETIZER on the room-service menu, and Gillian even went so far as to order another Zombie. While they were eating, she glanced at one of the magazines she'd bought in the gift shop.

"You know," she said, between bites of a Buffalo wing, "they say that a woman reaches her sexual peak in her thirties."

"How old are you?"

"Thirty-two."

"My, my." The grin he gave her was positively wicked.

"But men reach their sexual peak—"

"Impossible—"

"When they're eighteen— Kevin! Give me that magazine back!"

"I'm reaching my sexual peak right now."

MUCH LATER ON, they took a shower.

"Scrub my back," Kevin said.

Gillian picked up the soap, mouthing the request under her breath.

"What's that I hear?"

"Nothing." She began to lather his back, enjoying the play of muscles beneath her fingertips.

"That's nice. Could you rub my neck?"

She grinned, then slid her hands down his spine until she was touching his buttocks.

"Gillie—" There was a playfully warning tone to his voice.

"Yes?"

"That doesn't feel like my neck to me."

She slid her hands up to his hips, then around his front and down. She grinned as she realized he was getting aroused.

"You know what the penalty is for disobeying orders."

"And quite a penalty it is."

She shrieked as he pinned her against the cool tile of the shower stall, then kissed her until all she could do was put her arms around his neck and hold on.

When he finally stopped kissing her and she opened her eyes, he was looking down at her with the strangest expression. His lashes were spiky from the water, the intense expression in his deep blue eyes thrilled her, and his entire body seemed to disperse a tension that hadn't been there before.

"What?" she breathed.

His warm breath tickled her ear.

"I love you, Gillie."

She couldn't speak, her throat was so impossibly tight. Of all the ways she could have imagined it happening, she'd never considered him telling her in the shower.

"Me, too," she managed to squeak out.

"You love you, too?" Now he was teasing her again, mischief in those eyes, that cocky grin back in place.

She mock-punched his arm. "I love *you*!" Then her mouth trembled, her eyes filled and she laid her cheek against his chest as he stroked her wet hair.

THE BAR IN BERMUDA WAS POPULAR precisely because it had two crucial elements. A view of the ocean and a satellite dish.

And the bartender at this particular establishment, one Jim Lawrence, knew a man who had just had his heart broken when he saw one.

Dr. John Downey ordered another whiskey and water, then sat slumped morosely on his bar stool.

"She just left me," he said to no one in particular. "Hilary up and left me. She said she didn't want to spend her life with a man whose idea of a good time was fixing up broken-down animals."

The bartender placed the man's drink in front of him, along with a bowl of honey-roasted peanuts. "Good thing you found out now instead of later."

"She left me...."

He was a goner. *Women*. It was the same thing, every time. Jim couldn't even begin to count the number of times he'd heard this particular story.

The man in question, a pretty nice guy, was staying at the hotel next door. He didn't have access to a car, and Jim saw nothing wrong with letting the guy get quietly soused, then making sure he got to his room and slept it off.

Women.

He was polishing glasses when the tall, blond man and his wife came in. They looked like a pretty sophisticated couple, and Jim was surprised when they came up to the bar and ordered nothing more than fruit juice.

He was just finishing garnishing the glasses with pineapple spears when the news came on. He kept the dish tuned to the Los Angeles station. Jim had wanted to be an actor once, had even gone so far as to drive his beat-up Mustang to Hollywood. His short brush with fame had consisted of being a contestant on a game show and appearing naked in a few films he hoped had been destroyed in postproduction.

Now, living in Bermuda and tending bar was enough for him.

The perky blonde in her power suit cheerfully reported on the top news stories of the day. Dr. John ordered another drink. The tall blond man introduced himself as Charles MacKay. Jim introduced himself, and they discussed some of the attractions on the island. He found out that Charles and his wife, Stephanie, were heading back tomorrow morning, stopping at Disney World with their three children on their way back to Los Angeles.

"Then this newscast should make you folks feel right at home." Jim could smell a big tip coming from this couple. There was something about them that suggested money.

He was totally unprepared for the reactions of both men when the next news story came on.

The blonde barely missed a beat.

"And the search is still on for Spike, the feline spokescat for the Kitty Krunchies Kat Food Company. Though several people at the Merrill Advertising Agency have been following up phone leads, the big tabby has not shown up as of yet...."

"That's my cat!" Charles MacKay said with such force that Dr. John came out of his self-imposed funk and glanced up at the huge screen.

"I know that cat," he said after staring incredulously at the screen.

Jim looked up at the big screen, wondering if it was something in the water. Or perhaps the pineapple juice. All he could see was a large tabby cat in a commercial and a voiceover extolling the virtues of a particular brand of food.

"Ah, my girlfriend tried that stuff on Smokey and he didn't like it at all."

But neither man was listening to him.

"How do you know that cat?" MacKay asked Dr. John.

"I fixed his leg right before I left."

"Fixed his leg? What the hell was wrong with it?"

"Broken. Pretty standard procedure." He raised his glass to his lips, but MacKay stilled his arm.

"Who had the cat?"

"A friend of mine. She says she found him under a bush. His leg was pretty banged up so he couldn't get far."

"The poor thing. Does Kevin know?" This from Stephanie, who was gently rubbing her husband's arm, trying to calm him down.

And Jim, as he silently refilled their juice glasses and saw his tip flying out the window, wondered if the sun was especially strong today.

"Where is this friend of yours?" Charles asked.

"Panorama City. She's an older woman who takes in animals. And I *never* forget a furry face." Dr. John was still staring at the screen. It was completely filled with a closeup of the tabby cat's face, and a toll-free number appeared beneath it.

Charles turned to Jim. "Can you get me a phone right away?"

Jim snapped to attention, visions of a huge tip once again dancing in his mind. "Yes, sir!"

"Now, darling, don't get too upset," soothed Stephanie.

"You're sure that cat was Spike?" asked MacKay.

"Look at that little notch in his ear. And the scar below his left eye. I never forget a feline face," said Dr. John with all the dignity he could muster after four whiskey and waters.

Jim brought the cordless phone to Charles MacKay, Dr. John started to tell the sympathetic Stephanie about his breakup with Hilary the Heartless, and Jim stepped back, poured himself a generous glass of fruit juice, slipped in a double shot of rum, and decided to let the good times roll.

THEY PACKED MORE FUN into the next few days than Gillian believed possible. Kevin drove the Jeep out to the desert at sunset, to the Valley of Fire. The reddish earth, shaped by time and climate, looked like a giant's rock garden. The cliffs and crags seemed to come alive as the sun hit them, washing them with brilliant color before night swiftly fell. Then the stars blazed in the clear desert sky, and they lay in the back of the Jeep and tried to find various constellations.

They took in a show that was entirely made up of female impersonators. Las Vegas was filled with restaurants, and they tried a different one for each breakfast, lunch and dinner. Evenings, they drove the Jeep up and down the strip and people watched.

When they reached one of Las Vegas's numerous little chapels, Gillian couldn't take her eyes off the line of couples waiting to get married.

Marriage. She had entered her own with such high hopes, then seen them totally destroyed. Once the divorce had gone through, she'd vowed she would never repeat that experience. But a lot of that fear had come from the feeling that no man would ever want her because she could never make him happy.

Marriage to Kevin would be so easy. Though they were still very different people, with radically opposite ways of looking at life, he was so easygoing and tolerant of human frailties. Nothing at all like Bryant, who had to have everything his own way. He'd told her how to do everything, set limits on what was acceptable behavior and what was not, made her feel like she was never quite good enough.

Being with Kevin was so easy.

She glanced over at him and saw that his attention had been caught by the chapel, the same as hers had. Then she glanced away. And Gillian had the strangest feeling that to a man like Kevin MacClaine love and commitment would go hand in hand.

The thought didn't frighten her, and she was surprised by how easy it was when it felt right.

They stopped by a gift shop, and Gillian bought Ben a T-shirt, Corbin the tackiest ashtray she could find, then picked up several postcards. Kevin bought presents for his sisters, mother and father. While he wasn't looking, Gillian found a tiny ceramic tabby cat with a ribbon around its neck that spelled out Las Vegas in glittery letters. The cat's paw was on a slot machine, and the tiny bucket by its side was filled with coins.

They did check out a few more markets, and the remarks concerning Kitty Krunchies were depressingly familiar. It was a horrible, cheap product, even the cats could discern it wasn't something they wanted to be forced to eat. Gillian found herself talking to cat owner after cat owner, and she decided she was going to have a serious discussion with Ben about the product when she got back to the office.

Back in their hotel room, packages spread out all over one of the beds, they fell into the other one and Kevin admitted that he'd bought them tickets for one more show.

"What kind of show?"

"More dancing."

The evening was magical. Gillian had bought another dress, this one more casual. She wore the peach sundress for their evening out, and after eating dinner at Don the Beachcomber's, they went to the Tropicana's *Folies Bergere*, a lavish music-and-dance extravaganza.

Once back inside their room, lying in bed, she answered the question he had asked back in Palm Desert.

"I wanted to be a dancer."

"What happened?"

"It just didn't work out. I was taking dance classes as soon as I could walk, and I loved them. I loved the structure of it all, knowing what you were supposed to be doing, mastering it step-by-step. I used to always feel so free when I danced."

"And you didn't go after it professionally?"

"It was something that . . . just wasn't done. I was given those classes because my father thought I was clumsy. He didn't ever suspect it had turned into something so much more for me."

"You never talked to him about it?"

"I asked him to come to a recital once. Afterward we went to dinner and he gave me an entire critique. He didn't think I was very good. He told me he'd seen dancers in London and Paris who had far more—"

"It was a recital, not a professional performance!"

"I know that now. I didn't then. I never asked him to come to another recital after that."

"When did you stop taking classes?"

"About three years into my marriage. Bryant didn't like my spending so much time away from him."

He was silent then, staring at the ceiling of the hotel room, so still Gillian wondered what he was thinking.

"What was your dream?" he asked abruptly.

"I thought about being a dancer—"

"No, I mean the ultimate, the greatest fantasy you ever had. What did you really want?"

She smiled then as the memory came flooding back. "It's so classic. Me and a thousand other little ballerinas. I used to dream about dancing in *The Nutcracker*. My mother used to take me to see it every Christmas. It was one of the few things we did together, without my father or brothers. Once I started dancing, I wanted to be the Sugarplum Fairy."

It had been so important to her. She could almost see the child she'd been—small, wiry and intense, the clouds of copper hair pulled back in a restrained dancer's style. She'd loved everything about dancing, from the smell of the studio to the hours of work and aching muscles, the long, hot showers afterward, the sense of pure joy when a routine that had been baffling became easy and the next challenge presented itself. She had been able to pretend she was anyone when she'd danced. She'd been able to get outside herself and the endless restrictions that had always been placed on her.

Don't laugh too loudly, darling. Ladies don't.

Gillian, you must restrain yourself.

Why are you always so emotional?

Dancing had never betrayed her.

"So, some dream, huh?" She reached for his hand, feeling suddenly adrift. This man, this crazy, incredibly free spirit, had effortlessly asked for two of the secrets closest to her heart. He knew more about her than anyone did. And he made it all feel so safe.

"You could go back to class."

"At thirty-two?"

Now he caught her chin with his hand and the blue eyes were suddenly intense. "What, afraid you won't be the best in the class anymore? I bet you were, too."

Pain welled up inside her, pain for the dream that had been just within reach, if she'd had the courage.

"We can't all be like you, Kevin." She sat up, letting go of his hand. Wanting him to ease up for just a moment. Just until she got her equilibrium back.

Just until you can shovel it all back down and swallow it.

The thought caught her by surprise, then angered her. She faced him, feeling her cheeks start to sting with color.

"What do you mean, be like me?"

"Not everyone does exactly what they want all the time."

"Why not?"

"Because . . . sometimes there are other things you choose to do, sometimes things get in the way—"

"Sometimes you chicken out—"

"What is this? Are we going to spend the evening analyzing all my problems? Why don't we talk about you? Why aren't you ever afraid to go after what it is you really want?"

"Bravo," he said softly.

Her epithet was brief and explicit.

"So she gets angry, too."

She stood up and turned around to face him. To her horror, her hands were clenched into fists. And Gillian realized there was another side to passion, that emotions let loose in love also opened a floodgate of other, not so nice, feelings.

"What do you want, Gillie? It sure as hell isn't back at that office."

She uncurled her fingers and walked swiftly over to the window, trying to ignore him.

"I knew there was something else the minute I saw you screaming in the road. All that anger. All that passion. How long have you been holding it in?"

She felt as if someone had lit a match to tinder, and the flames were starting to flare, red-hot and hungry.

"What is it to you? *What do you want?*"

"I want us to talk about your midnight trips to the bathroom. About stomach pain so bad you have to curl up on the floor and press your cheek against the tile. About a life you've been living that's nothing but a lie—"

"Shut up!"

"How long are you going to keep hurting yourself?"

"Why is it any of your business what I do with my life?" She felt she was fighting for that life now, desperately trying to hold on to years of self-restraint, years of self-deception.

But Kevin kept at it, hammering away at her defenses until she felt there was nothing left to hide behind.

"What happens when this trip is over, Gillie? Are you going back to that office to sell cat food that's so bad you can't get most owners to force-feed it to their pets? Is that really what's going to make you happy?"

"It's important work—"

"It's *nothing* if it tears up your stomach and doesn't even let you sleep at night."

She launched herself at him then, and managed to punch him in the stomach before he grabbed both her wrists and wrestled her down to the bed.

"I hate you!"

"Good. Hate me if you can't hate that life of yours. Feel *something*, Gillie. Don't hold it all inside and let it tear up your guts."

She burst into tears and he held her tightly against him, letting go of her wrists and smoothing her hair away from her damp cheeks.

"I can't let it go, Gillie. Not after the other night. It killed me, seeing you in so much pain. And I know how much it hurts."

Her voice quavered from the force of her emotions. "How would you know? You're not afraid of anything."

"Everyone's afraid, Gillie."

"When were you ever afraid of anything?"

"A long time ago. Before Jeane and I divorced."

She couldn't fight him anymore, so she relaxed against him and stifled another sob. "Tell me," she whispered, her throat tight.

"Another time."

He was stroking her bare back, and the warmth of his hands seemed to melt the tension away. She turned her face against his shirtfront. He'd taken off his jacket when they'd returned to the room, along with his socks and shoes. Gillian closed her eyes, and one last tear seeped out, ran down her cheek and wet his shirt.

"I'm sorry, Gillie," he whispered. "But I hate seeing you hurting."

"This isn't hurting?" she whispered. His hands seemed warmer now, and she slipped her hand inside his shirt, resting it against the warmth of his chest.

"It hurts less than keeping it all inside."

She wasn't sure when it changed, but slowly comfort turned to passion, then they were kissing each other with a hungry intensity.

"You're so beautiful," he whispered, looking down at her.

"Red eyes and all?"

"Beautiful."

She'd never known lovemaking like this. Fierce, hungry, reaffirming the most primal of bonds. There wasn't time to take off all their clothing, he simply stripped off her panty hose and kicked off his pants. And this time, when she took him inside her, she cried out in wonder that something so physically fierce could feel so right. Then nothing else mattered as she was swept into total sensation.

HE WAS STANDING BY THE WINDOW, looking out over the lights, when she woke.

"Kevin?"

He walked over and sat down on the bed.

"I don't want to fight anymore," she whispered. "I want to be close."

"Me, too." He gathered her into his arms, and again she felt that incredible warmth.

"I was thinking," she said softly, rushing the words out of her mouth, "that we might be able to have a relationship if I changed and was a little bit more like you. I'm going to try, Kevin, just tell me what it is I have to do."

His hold on her tightened, then he said, "No, Gillie. I want to apologize for what I said. I had no right to do that to you, push you around that way. It took me a long time to make changes in my own life, and here I am expecting you to do it all overnight."

"But if I—"

"No, baby. No." And then, "I'm sorry."

"I am, too. I said some pretty nasty things."

"You just retaliated."

She snuggled closer. "You know more about me than anyone."

"I'm glad." He kissed the top of her head. "Remember when I said you needed a nickname?"

She nodded.

"You want one? I think I have it."

"Okay. I always wanted one when I was a kid. It seemed like all the really neat kids had them."

"Sugarplum. I'll always think of you as my Sugarplum."

"I love it. I love you."

"I love you too, Sugarplum. Just the way you are."

"You don't know where this woman lives." Charles MacKay wasn't angry with Dr. John Downey. He'd been in business too long and knew anger rarely did any good.

"She's always paid me in cash. I don't see her except when she brings animals into my office. And Dr. Gordon told me she hasn't been by the office since she brought Spike in."

"Does she own a television set?"

"I think it's broken."

"So basically, what you're telling me is that we have to wait until she comes into your office again, with Spike or another stray animal."

"That's about the size of it."

Charles glanced at Ben, seated at the other end of the oval table. "It doesn't look good. Shooting starts within the week. Even if we found Spike today, from what John says he wouldn't be in shape anyway."

"Maybe we could write around the accident," Ben mused. "Spike's character has always been a tough, street-smart cat. A broken leg would be in character."

"The leg's not going to be damaged permanently," Dr. John chimed in. "Once it heals, he should be good as new."

"Do we want to wait then, for Birdy to bring the cat in and for the leg to heal?" Charles asked.

"It's really up to you, Charles," Ben replied.

"I have an idea," Corbin offered confidently from his seat in the middle of the board room.

All three heads turned toward the younger man.

"Spike has a clearly defined persona. I don't think his having a broken leg is going to look good to the viewer. If Spike is such a tough guy, how did he get the broken leg in the first place? I was thinking that if we could use this opportunity to introduce another character, perhaps someone in Spike's immediate family, and have an alternate cat pitch the product, then Spike could heal up and be ready for the next shooting."

"He'll be ready in three months, won't he?" Charles MacKay asked the vet.

"He should be. He was a strong animal, if I'm remembering him correctly."

Ben nodded his head toward Corbin. "Go ahead with it. Find an alternate cat. If it's all right with you, Charles."

Charles Mackay didn't let so much as a flicker of body language betray him. Ben and Corbin watched him carefully until he said, "All right. Go ahead with it, make up a rough video and call me when it's done. In the meantime, keep an eye out for Spike and call me if anything happens."

BIRDY HESITATED as she reached for the phone.

It's time for him to go home.

Spike was sitting in the middle of her kitchen floor, grooming himself after his morning meal. The tabby was healing rapidly, and Birdy knew she was only deluding herself by hanging on to the cat.

Maybe Spike's owner had some kittens. Or she could go to the shelter and adopt one. As long as she made sure no one saw that she had a cat, she might be able to get away with having one.

I'll miss him.

He was a character. More like a dog than a cat. He followed her around the apartment, clearly enjoying her company. In the evening, when she read her usual biography, mystery or thriller in her favorite chair, he lay in her lap, up against her chest, his head on her shoulder. The deep, rumbling purr was soothing, and so much less lonely than silence.

You cannot keep putting it off. His people must be crazy with worry.

Blinking her eyes against the sudden moisture and knowing that once she called there was no turning back, Birdy picked up the receiver.

MADDIE, BEN'S SECRETARY, was typing a letter when the phone rang. Ben was out of the office on his lunch break. He'd decided to go to the doctor with Ashley for her monthly visit. Corbin was hot at work on his new Kitty Krunchies video. Maddie's only companion was Henry the chubby goldfish, who at this moment was swimming hopefully along the edge of the large bowl, waiting for a few fish flakes to be thrown in.

She picked up the phone on the first ring.

"The Merrill Agency, can I help you?"

"I have Spike." The older woman's voice quavered ever so slightly.

Maddie had been informed about the meeting with Dr. John Downey, and she knew exactly who this older woman probably was.

"Wonderful! Could I get your name and address? We'll send somebody out to your—"

"No. I want to know who his people are. Not the advertising agency. The people who own him. I want to give this cat directly to them."

There was the slightest bit of steel to her tone, and Maddie immediately respected it.

"That would be Kevin MacClaine, his trainer. I can give you his home number and you can contact him there. I understand he's on the road looking for Spike, but he calls in and checks his messages all the time, so he'll get in touch with you.''

''That would be the best thing,'' the woman said. She sounded relieved.

Maddie quickly flipped through her Rolodex, found Kevin's number and gave it to the woman. She had her read it back to her, then reassured the woman and urged her to call.

''I'll call right now. I think Spike misses his owner.''

''I'm sure he does. Thank you, Mrs.—''

''Birdy. Just Birdy.''

''Thank you, Birdy.''

And a split second after Maddie hung up the phone, she dialed Ben's beeper.

SAMANTHA COLLINS WAS TRYING to give Clementine the pig a much needed bath when the phone rang.

''Hello?'' She pushed her hair out of her eyes. It was a hellishly hot day, and the topknot that had been so secure when she'd started Clem's bath was sliding down her neck.

''Could I speak to Kevin MacClaine, please.'' The older woman's voice was crisp, completely no-nonsense.

''He's not here right now, but I'm his cousin. Could I take a message?''

Clementine chose that exact moment to let out a squeal of pig ecstasy. She loved baths, especially on hot days.

''What's that noise?'' Now the woman on the phone sounded worried.

"It's just Clem. I'm giving her a bath." Sam grinned. The explanations animal trainers had to come up with. "She's a pig."

"I thought as much. Mr. MacClaine has a pet pig?"

"And parrots and dogs and cats. And three horses out by the barn. He's thinking of getting a llama, and of course, there's Clem the pig. I could go on forever."

"Is Mr. MacClaine missing a cat?"

Sam caught her breath, then her heartbeat quickened. She'd had a feeling Spike was going to be coming home soon. She'd believed, as Kevin had, that the cat was fine and there was simply a delay in his finding his way back home.

"Yes, he is. A gray tabby. He's male and his name is Spike."

"I have Mr. MacClaine's cat, and I'd like to return him."

"Please, call him Kevin. 'Mr. MacClaine' makes me think of his father. What happened? Is Spike all right?"

"I found him in the bushes by my apartment. His leg was broken, but I took him to my vet—"

"Bless you!"

"—And he's going to be just fine. My television was broken, or I would have returned him sooner."

"I can't tell you how happy Kevin is going to be. He's in Las Vegas, I could give you his number." Sam hesitated for just a second. She'd grown up trusting her instincts, and her instincts were telling her this was an older woman, probably on a tightly fixed income.

"Why don't you give me your number and I'll call Kevin and have him call you? What's your name?"

"Birdy."

"I'm Samantha."

Clementine let out another squeal and Sam glanced over to see what had captured the pig's attention. Ryan, her husband, was leaning in the doorway, a lazy grin on his face. She stuck out her tongue at him, knowing how amusing he undoubtedly thought she and Clem looked.

He walked into the bathroom and hunkered down on the floor, then began to scratch a delighted Clementine behind her ears. The pig started to snort.

Birdy gave her her home phone number, then said softly, "I had a pet pig when I was a girl."

"Did you grow up on a farm?" Sam asked.

"Yes."

"I did, too. More like a compound." She covered the mouthpiece of the phone and whispered, "We've found Spike."

Ryan gave her a thumbs-up and continued to scratch Clem.

"Thank you, Samantha, for calling Kevin."

"Thank *you* Birdy. I'm sure Kevin will be inviting you over for dinner or something. He'll think of a unique way to thank you, that's just the way he is."

"Oh. That would be wonderful. Goodbye, dear."

"Goodbye, Birdy."

Sam hung up the phone, gave her husband a kiss, then said, "It's Spike. I know it. He broke his leg, that's why it took so long to find him. And her television—"

Ryan silenced her with another kiss, then said, "I knew that old reprobate was fine. How's Kevin doing with that woman?"

"Gillian Sommers."

"The redhead."

Sam grinned. "They'll end up getting married."

"How can you be so sure?" Clem snorted and Ryan continued to scratch her behind her ears.

"Because it was hate at first sight."

"Are you implying—"

"That the men in your family love a challenge? No, I'm not implying it, I'm saying it's a fact."

"So Kevin's going to bite the dust."

"He was long overdue. Now, this little piggy needs to finish her bath, then I've got to take care of the parrots and we'll just make it to Jo's recital."

"Don't forget to call Kevin," he teased.

"I'll have to give this Gillian some tips or she'll be crushed by her fighting Irishman."

"You love it."

"Wash the pig."

THEY WERE ASLEEP IN BED when the phone rang. Gillian heard Kevin talking, and he seemed to be speaking from far away, the words were muffled. He hung up the phone, then she felt his hand on her shoulder, gently nudging her awake.

"They've found him."

"What?" She sat up in bed, all thoughts of sleep cleared from her brain.

"They've found Spike."

Chapter Nine

They'd crossed the state line into California before she worked up the courage to ask Kevin what had been on her mind from the beginning of their journey back home.

"What do you see happening to us, Kevin? Where do you see this going?"

He was silent for such a long time she thought the worst and steeled herself for his reply.

So you were a bimbo for a while. Not just for a while—for the best time in your life.

Then he said it.

"Forever, Gillie. Forever and ever, if you want it."

She couldn't stop looking at him; she had to get closer. Throwing her arm around his shoulder, she snuggled up as best she could with two bucket seats.

"Oh, Kevin."

He grinned, then gave her a quick kiss, his eyes still on the road ahead. "I think, Sugarplum, that this is the beginning of the best time we've ever had."

BIRDY'S APARTMENT WAS QUIET, small and cool. Gillian sat and sipped her tea as she watched Kevin change the batteries in Birdy's smoke alarm.

The reunion of man and cat had been surprisingly emotional. Spike's eyes had widened, then he had clumsily bounded up to Kevin and meowed until he'd been picked up. Now he sat firmly on the chair Kevin was standing on as he fiddled with the smoke alarm.

And Birdy was watching them, a brave smile pasted on her tired face.

She's lonely, Gillian thought suddenly. Birdy was a good woman and she didn't deserve to be lonely. But Gillian had no idea what to do.

Kevin, amazingly deft when it came to people's feelings, came up with the perfect solution.

"Well," he said, standing in Birdy's doorway with Spike hanging over his shoulder and looking blissful, "I'll never be able to thank you enough for what you did for Spike, Birdy."

Gillian felt her nose begin to sting, her throat tighten. What happened once they left? It was clear Spike had been good company and a comfort to the old woman.

"Anyone would have."

"Anyone wouldn't have," Kevin corrected her softly. "That's what made what you did so special."

Birdy smiled then, but Gillian could see her eyes glistening with unshed tears.

"There is one more thing, though," Kevin said.

And Gillian was reminded of the young mother and her children outside Palm Desert, of how hungry the woman had been just to talk. And how Kevin had spent so much time in her kitchen.

"Yes?" Birdy said.

"I'm looking for someone to help me out at the compound—you probably wouldn't be interested—"

"Interested in what, young man?"

"Well, I'm outside most of the time, and I'd like to have someone kind of keep an ear on the phone, maybe watch the animals inside, help me when they're sick. Just general-duty stuff. I need someone with that special feel for animals, and I know you have it because of what you did for Spike."

"How many hours a week would you need me?" Birdy asked, a sparkle of life coming into her blue eyes. And Gillian set her teacup down, biting her lip to keep from crying.

She'd never loved Kevin more.

"You could set your own hours. Oh, and you'd have to like children, because Samantha sometimes brings Johanna over. She can get into trouble quicker than any kid I know."

"I like little girls," Birdy said, memories behind her eyes.

"You think you might like to give it a try?"

As if in answer, Spike meowed.

"See, even Spike thinks it's a good idea."

"When would you need me?"

Was it Gillian's imagination, or did Birdy already seem to be standing up straighter?

"Tomorrow morning. The blacksmith's coming to trim the horses' hooves, and just once I'd like to be out there with him instead of inside trying to get the parrots to stop screaming."

"Parrots." Birdy looked worried. "I don't have a lot of experience with birds."

"Nothing to it. The gang I have is a bunch of softies. And I think we can even find transportation for you. There's a guy who's working with the horses for the next few months, I'm sure we can arrange some sort of car pool, he drives right by on his way out. I'll have him give you a call tonight."

"That would be fine." Birdy walked briskly up to Kevin's side, then stroked Spike's head gently. "So, I'll see you in the morning, won't I, Spike?"

Spike only purred.

"I can't thank you enough, Birdy."

Her eyes were twinkling. "I'll see you tomorrow."

STRANGELY ENOUGH, now that Kevin was finally dropping her by her town house, Gillian didn't want to go there.

"Don't give me that look with those big green eyes. I just thought you might like some time to yourself before work tomorrow."

She sighed, knowing he was right, but hating to leave him. "I have to see Ben first thing in the morning."

"I'll pick you up tomorrow night. Our first official date in the city. Anything you want."

"Something blissfully ordinary. Maybe dinner and a movie."

"Sounds good."

He dropped her off, carried her bags inside, Spike still riding on his shoulder.

"What time are you finished with work?"

"I'll be done at five."

"What, no more late nights?" His blue eyes were teasing.

"No more work for this girl. I'm going to learn to play."

"I like your attitude, Sugarplum. Let me know what Ben says about Spike. You can call me anytime, I'll write down my beeper number. That way if I'm outside, you can still get me."

"I don't want to bother you."

"I want to be bothered. Twenty-four-hour access, Gillie. Use it."

He kissed her, several times, then was gone.

She watched the Jeep pull away, then walked back into her living room and sat down, tucking her feet beneath her. Her bags were strewn out over the rug, and as her eyes fell on one of the gaudy plastic bags with Las Vegas emblazoned across it, she remembered she'd forgotten to give Kevin the ceramic tabby cat.

She'd forgotten everything when he'd told her they'd found Spike.

Forever and ever.

She smiled to herself, then, determined not to turn into a daydreaming slug and neglect everything she had to do, she picked up her bags and headed for the laundry room.

"Who did it to you, Spike?" Kevin asked.

But Spike, lying contentedly on his master's stomach, didn't answer. He merely stared at his owner with those inscrutable green-gold eyes.

Kevin was sure someone had helped Spike leave the compound. Someone who had something to gain. At first he'd considered letting it go, now that Spike was back and in one piece. But seeing the formerly vibrant animal limping around the compound had made his normally calm temper start to flare.

Thank God for Birdy. Without her, Spike wouldn't have survived. It was tough enough being a stray, let alone a stray with a broken leg.

Kevin had paid her back in full for the vet bill, even over her protestations that her vet hadn't charged her anything. And he'd liked her. Liked her enough to offer her a job he hadn't even known existed until he'd decided to make it up.

The screen door slammed and Kevin knew it had to be Samantha. She was one of the only people he'd trusted with a key. They were used to being each other's backup when the other had an emergency and couldn't tend the animals.

"Kevin?"

"In the bedroom."

Sam and Johanna came into the bedroom, and Sam's eyes lit up when she saw Spike.

"It really was him!"

"The one and only. Oh, if you know anyone who wants a cat, I have two coming up from Huntington Beach tomorrow. A tabby kitten and a calico."

Sam smiled. "I know you, you'll end up keeping them."

Kevin grinned. "Probably. Bring Johanna by tomorrow, I also have a new employee starting on. She has a soft spot for children." He explained about Birdy while Sam petted Spike and Johanna asked where Clementine was.

"Now to the good stuff," Sam said, sitting down on the edge of the water bed. "When are you seeing Gillie again?"

"Tomorrow night. Dinner and a movie."

"I love it. Just like normal people."

"I'm meeting her at her office."

"Where is it?"

"Century City."

"You'll have to dress up."

He hadn't thought of that. Kevin, forehead wrinkled, did a quick mental inventory of what he had in his closet. His one suit was too formal. But all he had besides that were jeans, jeans and more jeans. Worn jeans. Jeans with holes in them. And T-shirts. An outstanding collection of T-shirts. Cowboy boots.

The hick from the valley dating Miss Century City.

"What are you doing right now, Sam?"

"Now? Talking to you."

"I mean later in the day."

"Jo and I have to be home around seven. We didn't really have anything planned—"

"Come shopping with me. Help me pick out some clothes for tomorrow."

She didn't even crack a smile, and Kevin thought what a wise man his cousin Ryan was. Beauty, brains and a healthy dose of compassion for a foolish guy who desperately wanted to make a good impression.

"There has to be a mall somewhere around here. How about it, Jo, you want to go to the mall with Kevin?"

Johanna's dark green eyes were mutinous, her lower lip thrust out. "I want to see Clem."

"We can see Clem when we get back."

"I'll buy you an ice-cream cone, Johanna. We can go see the puppies at the pet shop." Kevin wasn't above a dose of good old-fashioned bribery. He knew a tough training assignment when he saw one.

Sam merely rolled her eyes.

Johanna considered the deal, then made a lightning fast decision. "Okay. But we have to bring some ice cream back for Clem."

GILLIAN HAD SHOWERED, finished three loads of wash and was putting her new, post-Kevin clothing away when she took a good look at her closet.

It was all quite appropriate for work, but not quite right for dinner and a movie.

Especially with Kevin. He'd never been that fond of her business suits.

She threw the rest of her freshly laundered clothing on her bed, grabbed her purse and headed out the door.

THERE WAS, SAMANTHA DECIDED later that afternoon, nothing quite as charming as a vulnerable man in love.

"How does this look?" The casual tone Kevin had adopted was completely at odds with the look in his eyes.

"Nice. But we can do better. Put on the blue sweater, but keep the pants."

When Kevin obediently turned and headed back to the dressing room, she knew he'd been bit bad. Most men barely tolerated wasting time shopping for clothes, let alone dressing up. Every time Ryan had to wear a tuxedo, he'd start complaining several days before the event. As a director, he was used to jeans and sweats.

And Kevin was even worse. One good thing to be said for animals, they didn't care how you looked.

"What do you think?"

He looked fabulous. The gray pants were pleated, the sweater was a mixture of blues, grays and black.

"That's it. You'll be fighting her off all evening."

The look he gave her made her start to laugh.

"Maybe I should get another sweater or something. I can't wear this every time we go out."

"I should have you talk to Ryan. He has shirts he wore in college. If I even contemplated throwing them out, we'd be headed for divorce."

"Ice cream?" Johanna piped up hopefully.

Sam swept her daughter up into her lap and gave her a hug. "In three more sweaters and two more pairs of pants."

"Mommy, you talk funny."

Kevin and Samantha merely laughed.

"YOU'RE SURE YOU WANT ME to layer it?" Roberto was incredulous, and Gillian could see why. He'd been after her for months to layer her thick mane of hair, but she'd stalled him, insisting on only the most tame of trims at each visit.

"I just want a look that's a little more...carefree."

"You're going to love it," he assured her.

And she did. With two inches taken off the bottom and layers cut throughout, the natural wave in her hair was released. It looked younger, fuller—and definitely sexier.

"Anything else?"

Gillian thought of the mountains of bags stowed in the trunk of her BMW. The salesladies at the local mall had loved her today; she'd gone completely wild, buying clothes, shoes, earrings, perfume, soaps and lotions. It was funny how she'd felt she was finally expressing a part of herself that had been buried for a long time.

"Some of that eyeshadow, a new blush and that crazy hair bow in the front display case."

"I approve!" Roberto said. "What happened, darling? Did you get lucky over the weekend?"

"Better than lucky. He's wonderful."

"Well, if he has a friend, send him over."

SHE SPREAD everything out on her bed, tried it all on again and settled on black leggings, a leopard-look sweater and a gold metallic bow.

He bought Johanna a gallon of vanilla ice cream, which she promptly took back to the compound and shared with Clementine and Spike.

She lazed in a scented bath and thought of him, weaving some decidedly erotic fantasies.

He lazed in his hammock after Sam and her daughter left, missed Gillie, and thought of how their evening was going to end.

She thought of calling him.

He thought of calling her.

She decided he might need some privacy.

He didn't want her to think he was crowding her.

And both of them walked around in that rarefied state of stupefied bliss reserved for the very much in love.

"YOU LOOK WONDERFUL!"

Corbin was waiting in her office as Gillian had expected. There wasn't much he ever missed, and she was touched that he'd thought to welcome her back with a bouquet of flowers on her desk.

He laughed when he unwrapped the ashtray and promised it would hold a place of honor on his desk.

"So, MacClaine found the cat. Amazing, isn't it?"

"If it hadn't been for Birdy, I doubt Spike would have survived."

"But he can't do the commercial with that leg of his."

"Not for a while, no."

"Have you talked to Ben yet?"

"Should I?"

"We're having a big meeting tomorrow. Mac-Claine's bringing in the cat and we'll be discussing alternate ways of marketing the cat food."

Gillian reached over and made a note on her note pad concerning discussing the fact that Kitty Krunchies was not a favorite among the feline set.

"I can't get over it. You look like you spent a week at La Costa."

"I had a good time." It was all she would say. She didn't really feel comfortable discussing her personal life with Corbin.

Ben was a different story.

"You did it on purpose, didn't you?"

"Can you blame me? Gillie, you look terrific."

"Thanks, Ben. For seeing what I couldn't see, and it was all right in front of my nose."

"My pleasure."

"How's Ashley?"

"Just fine."

He spent the next hour catching her up on what had happened in the office during her absence, and Gillian told him about the report she was going to prepare concerning her field research on the Kitty Krunchies line.

"It's horrible food, Ben. That's all I heard, in every market I was in."

"Strange. MacKay's products are usually outstanding." He was silent for a moment, sitting back in his chair, his fingers steepled. Gillian, from long experience, knew better than to interrupt his train of thought.

Soon enough, she knew Ben would make his point.

"I'm going to check into this, Gillie. If what you say is true, my instincts tell me there's a strong chance MacKay doesn't know what's going on with the cat food."

"I'll tell him everything I've told you."

"I think that will be necessary."

She spent the rest of the day busily compiling her report and watching the clock out of the corner of her eye. At quarter to five, she asked Maddie to keep an eye out for Kevin, then went into the executive washroom to change into her new clothes.

She decided against the bow, liking the look of her new cut loose around her shoulders. Adding just a little more makeup to what she normally wore to the office, Gillian gave herself a critical once-over, and decided she'd do.

She was barely back in her office when Maddie buzzed her.

"He's here."

He looked wonderful, but she felt suddenly shy, seeing him in a totally different environment.

Maddie, ever quick to flirt with an attractive man, had obviously already introduced herself.

"And this," she said, indicating the fishbowl on her desk, "is Henry, Gillian's fish."

Kevin was merciless during their elevator ride down to the garage.

"So all this time I was up against a fish?"

"I just thought a little healthy competition was in order."

"That's right, 'he swims.' 'We hang around the town house a lot.' I guess you couldn't go far on a date with Henry."

"Samantha was married."

"I never implied we were an item."

"But by what you left out you made me believe the two of you were involved."

He shook his head. "A fish. I was jealous of a fish."

They drove their separate cars to the Century City Mall, then met up at the Cineplex. With fourteen different theaters to choose from, Gillie was surprised they agreed on a picture so quickly. They chose a typical cop buddy film with a twist—the partner was a German Shepherd.

Afterward they ate at the deli near the theater. Kevin knew the man who had trained the dog, and they argued the merits of the film, pro and con, discussed the difficulty of training animals for film and talked a little about the next day's meeting.

"Spike won't be working for a while. I want him to recover completely. He's never minded doing the commercials, he's got a pretty outgoing personality, but I just want to make sure he's in good shape before he works again."

"I don't blame you. I'm sure Ben and Mr. MacKay aren't going to expect Spike to spring back into action."

"I think they just want to take a look at him to reassure themselves that he's still alive."

They drove to her town house, still in separate cars.

"So this time I get to see the bedroom," Kevin teased her as they walked in the front door. "But I have to ask—where did Henry sleep?"

"His bowl is usually right on the kitchen counter. He likes a view of the television."

Afterward they lay in bed and talked.

"I brought you a set of keys to the compound, in case you ever need to get in when I'm not there."

She knew it was a first, crucial step to combining their households, and her heartbeat quickened.

"I have an extra set I'll give you in the morning."

"I like your hair. It's cute. It suits you."

"Thanks. I liked your sweater."

He kissed the side of her neck.

"You smell great."

"It's new perfume. I picked it out for you."

"Good."

She rubbed his hair-roughened leg with her foot.

"Gillie, we're both going to be dead tomorrow."

Her foot continued its sensuous caress.

"Why do I get the feeling you're going to have your wicked way with me?"

She laughed, then sighed her pleasure as he lifted her up on top of him.

GILLIAN COULDN'T HAVE SAID exactly when she noticed it, but Corbin was clearly nervous.

"Do you think this is enough of a power tie?"

"I'm not even sure what that is," she confessed. "But let me straighten it for you."

Corbin *was* nervous. He had a video tucked beneath his arm, and Gillian knew he'd worked overtime several nights in order to have his alternate commercial for Kitty Krunchies ready for this particular meeting.

She'd known when she came to work for the Merrill Advertising Agency that Corbin was distantly related to Ben. And she also knew Corbin felt the pressure of nepotism every day, believed he had to work just that much harder than anyone else so as not to let Ben down. He practically worshipped the man, and Gillian had always been aware Corbin was slightly envious of the relationship she had with Ben.

She respected Corbin. He'd never hinted, in any conversation, that he was envious. An intelligent man, Corbin was the consummate team player. Yet Gillian, that morning, sensed Corbin didn't seem to believe he had what it took to do an outstanding job.

"You'll be fine," she said, patting the knot in his tie. "I'm sure Ben and Charles will love your idea."

"We'll see," he said quietly, his mouth tense.

She felt suddenly sorry for him. He did seem to have to work harder than some of the other executives in the firm, and she knew he considered himself a second runner-up.

A sad self-perception, but there was nothing she could do.

They were already in the meeting room when Kevin walked in, dressed in a suit and tie. He was carrying Spike in a plastic cat kennel, and Gillian was amazed at how calm the large tabby was. But then, Spike had been in the business for quite a few years.

Kevin's eyes were warm when they met hers, but he didn't acknowledge her in any other way. She was glad he'd chosen to keep their relationship private.

Charles MacKay came straight to the point.

"Well, let's see Spike."

Kevin carefully lifted Spike out of his carrier. The cat seemed uneasy, which was unusual because he was the consummate performer. He crouched down on the table and let out a pitiable yeowl.

"Come on, Spike. What's the matter?" Kevin snapped his fingers gently, and Spike slunk toward him at the empty side of the table.

Kevin picked him up and, as he stroked the cat's head, said quietly, "He's never behaved this way before." He walked down to the far end of the table, and Spike seemed to visibly relax as the distance grew between him and the other people in the room besides Kevin.

He set Spike on top of the oval table. The hair on his shaved leg was growing in, but it was still noticeably shorter than the surrounding hair. Kevin snapped his fingers, and Spike followed him as he walked alongside the table. There was the slightest limp, but the cat was still a proud animal.

Spike walked the length of the table again, then Kevin picked him up and sat down in his designated chair.

"He can't do the commercial with that leg," MacKay said.

"No." Kevin agreed.

Gillian remained silent. Something about the way Spike had behaved made her uneasy. Yet Kevin had remained the professional. She was fascinated by this completely new side of him, in a suit and tie and totally at ease in the business world. How could she have ever thought of this man in such a narrow way? He wasn't a dumb jock, and he was certainly nothing like Bryant.

She smiled, proud of him. Proud he was hers.

"Will he be all right?" MacKay asked, and Gillian detected more than a professional interest in the question.

Kevin must have as well, because the expression in his blue eyes warmed.

"He will. Give him a couple of months and he'll be as good as new."

"How did he get out of that compound of yours?"

"I'm not really sure. I have a theory, but it's speculation."

"Go ahead."

"I think someone stole him."

"That's ridiculous!" Corbin exclaimed.

And Gillian leaned forward, a terrible suspicion growing inside her.

"It's just a suspicion," Kevin said softly, his gaze intent on Corbin.

There was a short silence, then Ben said, "Charles, we have a few alternate ideas for the Krunchies campaign, if you'd like to see them." He turned toward Kevin. "Mr. MacClaine, you don't have to stay if you don't want to. We'll certainly be contacting you once Spike is well."

"I'd like to stay if you don't mind."

"Fine."

Corbin's video was inserted into the VCR, and Gillian leaned forward, hoping against hope that Corbin's idea was good. He was creatively erratic, and she'd sat through many a presentation totally unsuitable to the product.

"I thought," Corbin began, "we could try and capture a market that's more...upscale. They have the most disposable income. Spike's persona appeals to the blue-collar worker, but I think if we spin a few characters off of Spike with—how shall I say it—a broader range, it will ensure the Kitty Krunchies Kat Food line will continue to enjoy increased profits."

MacKay nodded his head, encouraging Corbin to continue.

"Remember that ad campaign we did for Heritage Dog Food, with that bulldog? Sales went through the roof."

"That bulldog," Kevin cut in suddenly, "was a media hero before the ad campaign was aired. He'd inherited billions of dollars. I knew the woman who took care of him and she almost got herself killed in the process. She runs one of the most successful animal agencies in the state. I don't see how you can compare your proposed campaign to the Heritage ads."

Gillian was stunned. Kevin had a point, and he'd expressed it succinctly. But knowing him as she did, she was able to detect the tiniest note of hostility toward Corbin.

Again, the same terrible suspicion flooded her, centering in her stomach. Unconsciously, her hands clenched into fists in her lap.

"He has a point, Corbin," Ben said.

Corbin paused for a moment, and it seemed to Gillian he looked like he'd had the wind knocked out of him.

"Well," he said finally. "I think I'll just let the video speak for itself."

The lights dimmed and the video began to play.

The background was familiar enough. Most of Spike's commercials were shot in a back lot that looked like a Brooklyn neighborhood. This same neighborhood was on the tape, and as the music began to swell, Gillian recognized the distinct beat of Billy Joel's song "Uptown Girl."

A white Persian, delicate, fluffy, sporting a diamond collar, was walking down the sidewalk, crowds of cats sitting on the brownstone steps she passed.

And the singer sounded exactly like Billy Joel, except the words were different.

Kit-ty Krunch
Is the perfect thing to have for lunch,
And for breakfast and for dinner too,
Every cat knows it's a dream come true.

Now the white Persian was eating some Kitty Krunchies out of a crystal bowl. The camera panned back, showing a few of the other cats eating.

And when they eat it, they know it's a pri-i-ize,
And ev'ry kitty will choose, if he's wi-i-ise,
The food that tastes so good,
Just like a

Cat food should,
Yes, it's Kit-ty Kru-unch...

By the end of the video, all the cats were eating Kitty Krunchies, and the white Persian was a true heroine.

The lights came up. MacKay was brooding, but then you could never tell what he thought right away.

"It's cute," Gillian volunteered.

"It's got possibilities," Ben said.

"Where did you get the cat?" Kevin asked.

"From another trainer," Corbin said.

Gillian's stomach was going wild.

"What's his name?"

"Her name." Now Corbin was beginning to look more confident, and Gillian hoped against hope that what she'd suspected was just another product of her overdeveloped imagination.

"What's her name?" Kevin leaned forward in his chair, his palms flat on the table. He'd put Spike back in his carrier when the video began.

"Samantha Collins. She specializes in cats."

Gillian thought Kevin would be pleased a friend of his was getting work. Instead, the look in his blue eyes was murderous.

"*Big* cats. Sam specializes in big cats."

Now Corbin looked visibly uneasy.

"What did you do, look her up in the directory just so you'd have a name to throw out?"

"Look, MacClaine, I don't know what you're trying to imply."

Kevin's next words stunned them all.

"Take off your shirt."

"I beg your pardon," Corbin said sharply.

"You know what I'm after. Take off your shirt or I'll do it for you."

"Really, this is the most ridiculous—"

Gillian jumped in her seat as Kevin reached across the conference table and grabbed Corbin's tie, the tie she'd so carefully straightened not even an hour ago.

"Off."

"Mr. MacClaine, I think you'd better sit down," Ben said, the warning clear in his voice.

Then pandemonium erupted as Kevin leaped across the table and the two men exploded into a fight. Somewhere in the middle of the struggle, Kevin decked Corbin and he slumped to the floor. Gillian clamped her hand over her mouth to stifle a scream, then stunned realization flooded her as Kevin deftly removed first Corbin's suit jacket, then his shirt.

He stood up, his breath coming in gasps, his muscled chest rising and falling with exertion.

"You son of a— I knew Spike wouldn't leave without a struggle."

Across Corbin's arms, startling against his pale skin, were the most wicked cat scratches Gillian had ever seen.

Before anyone could say anything else, Kevin picked up the cat carrier containing Spike and walked out of the conference room.

Gillian started to go after him, but Ben caught her arm.

She looked up at the man who had been more of a father to her than her own and knew that even if her actions disappointed him, she had to go after Kevin.

"Ben," she said softly. He let go then, and she knew he had seen it all in her eyes.

Kevin was waiting by the elevator, Spike's carrier by his side, when she reached him. His body was tense, his blue eyes angry.

"Why don't you just get back to your meeting?"

She shook her head. "It's not all that important anymore. Where are you going?"

"Home. If Ben or MacKay want to work with Spike they're going to have to get rid of that guy."

She touched his upper arm, feeling the tight muscles. "Corbin's as good as fired."

He shook his head, his expression still grim. "I'd like to throw him into a jungle, make him wander around and hunt for food. And I'd bet money no one would take him in."

She knew Corbin's intent hadn't been to kill Spike. The man was incompetent, and her instincts told her he'd simply gotten in something over his head. But it didn't excuse him from facing the consequences of what he'd done. As close as she and Corbin were, something inside her had died when she'd seen the scratches on his arms and realized he'd been instrumental in Spike's disappearance.

"I'll never feel the same way about him again," she said.

Kevin's gaze was steady on her face, and she realized that this was a man who had to have utter loyalty, who would want his woman to side with him completely. There was no fence-sitting when it came to a nature as passionate as Kevin's.

"I'm sorry, Gillie," he said suddenly, reaching up and sliding his hand around the back of her neck, then kissing her. The elevator door opened, then shut again before he let her go.

"It's okay."

"I didn't mean to ruin things for you. I just—I saw red."

"I know."

He grinned then, slowly, that grin that reminded her of a cat who'd eaten the canary. "Get back in there and tell MacKay his cat food's only fit for compost."

She laughed then, kissed him again, leaning into his strength. "I've written up a pretty incredible report," she admitted.

"Give 'em hell." The elevator door opened again, and this time Kevin stepped inside. "I'll call you tonight."

She nodded, then watched as the elevator slid shut. Then Gillian took a deep breath, trying to calm her stomach.

Easy.

The pains were just barely there, then she felt them starting to fade. She took another breath, then another.

Gone.

Smiling, her mind made up, Gillian started back toward the conference room.

Make it good, she said to herself. *After all, it's going to be your swan song.*

"SO YOU SEE, Mr. MacKay, it isn't even that good a cat food."

Charles MacKay's composure was rattled. It was a first.

"I don't understand it. We hired a team of veterinarians to make sure it was the best it could possibly be. I don't understand how what you say could be true."

"I asked people in markets in Palm Desert, Huntington Beach and Las Vegas. I called several veterinarians in the Los Angeles area. It may have started out as a first-class cat food, but it's not anymore."

Gillian loved a good argument, and she found herself sticking to her position, not giving an inch.

"I can see why Ben's glad to have you on his team, Ms. Sommers."

"Thank you."

"I think I'll have to have a little chat with my son tonight, check up on how he's running the business."

Afterward Gillian asked Ben if she could go home. And as she was driving to her town house, she thought of how the Gillian Sommers of even a month ago wouldn't have thought to leave early after a meeting like that. She would have worked through any upsetting emotions she might have had.

Now all she could think of was talking to Kevin.

She phoned him when she got home, but his answering machine picked up. Gillian left a message, then went into the kitchen and poured herself a glass of juice. She hadn't eaten breakfast that morning. Kevin had left early in order to return to the compound and get Spike. She'd been too upset for lunch.

She'd barely drunk half the glass when the pains started.

They were different this time, fast and hard. Gut wrenching. The glass slipped from her fingers and she watched, as if from far away, as juice exploded all over her white kitchen floor.

By the time she was halfway to the bathroom, she was crawling.

The cabinet...

She couldn't stop coughing. There was a tickle in her chest and she was coughing so violently she had to stop and lie down in the hallway.

This isn't the same . . .

She blocked the thought out of her mind, concentrated instead on how good it was going to feel to lie on the cool bathroom floor. She could wring out a washcloth and cover her face with it.

The meeting. The meeting upset you . . .

Once in the bathroom she swallowed some Pepto Bismol, then wet a washcloth and put it over her face. She tried to breathe, but the pain was so bad she couldn't take a complete breath.

Easy. Easy. It'll go away. It always goes away . . .

She started to cough, and when she sucked in air in a reflex action, the washcloth felt like it was smothering her. Clawing it away from her face, she lay on the bathroom floor, staring up at the ceiling and panting. She could feel another cough coming, a violent one, and she put the washcloth over her mouth and felt the cough explode out of her.

Gillian closed her eyes as she pressed the wet washcloth over her mouth. This was worse than any pain she'd had before. Her legs were starting to shake and she felt dizzy.

Get to bed . . .

That was the answer. If she just lay down for an hour or so, it would pass. It always passed. Gillian took a deep breath, resisting the urge to cough again and opened her eyes.

And saw blood all over the washcloth.

Chapter Ten

She had a moment of crystal clear clarity before panic threatened to overwhelm her. Gillian stared at the washcloth, then dropped it on the bathroom floor. The pain was still sharp, causing the next breath she drew in to sting her nose. Her mind cleared again, and she knew that no matter how afraid she was of doctors and what they might tell her, she had to get to a hospital.

She got to her knees, slowly, fighting pain with every movement. Hooking her arms around the sink, she hauled herself up, then wished she hadn't looked in the mirror. Her face was deathly pale, her green eyes dull with pain. In vivid contrast a thin trickle of blood stood out at the corner of her mouth.

Reaching for reserves of strength she didn't realize she possessed, Gillian stumbled out into the hallway, then fumbled for her car keys and purse on the small table. The pain was coming in pulsating waves, and she leaned up against the wall, closing her eyes and pressing a palm to her wet forehead.

A little farther... The car...

As soon as she thought the words, she knew she wouldn't be able to drive.

Phone. The nearest one was in the kitchen, and she pulled herself along into that room, then held on to the counter as she walked its length and picked up the receiver.

She'd never really had anyone to depend on when she was sick before. When she'd still been in private school during the day, the housekeeper had come and picked her up if she was sick, so she'd gotten used to relying on no one at an early age. But now, fingers shaking as she pulled Kevin's beeper number out of her purse, Gillian knew she had someone she could count on.

The cough caught her by surprise, and she barely had time to cover her mouth. When she drew her hand away and saw the blood, she wiped her hand on the counter reflexively, trying to distance herself from it in any small way she could. The crimson stain was brilliant against the white tiles, and her eyes filled with frightened tears.

The slip of paper had fallen on the counter. She picked it up, reached for the phone and tried to dial the number. But another cough caught her, and the receiver slipped out of her fingers and banged against the counter.

She could feel the exact moment when she started to come apart, and she'd never wished for anything in her life as hard as she wished Kevin was with her at that instant.

"Gillie?"

She looked up, having trouble focusing her eyes because of the pain. Kevin, a shocked look on his face, was in front of her, then next to her, his arms around her. She leaned into his strength, breathing in the scent of him in short little breaths. Relieved tears filled her eyes, as her mind tried to comprehend what she'd seen.

He's here. He's here. Everything's going to be all right....

She coughed again, trying to cover her mouth, not wanting to get blood all over his shirt. But before she could do anything more, he was carrying her outside and settling her into his Jeep, buckling her seat belt. His touch was so gentle. Her eyes were closed, so she couldn't see the strained look on his face, the fear in his eyes.

"It's all right, Gillie. It's going to be all right."

Then they were moving, and whenever he wasn't shifting gears, Kevin held her hand tightly.

SHE LAY IN THE HOSPITAL BED, deeply aware of the absence of pain.

A bleeding ulcer. A special diet. She'd been shocked at the diagnosis, then realized how stubborn and foolish she'd been, trying to treat the beginning of the condition for years. A combination of her own fear of doctors and the sense of having no time had been the excuse she'd given herself for resisting professional treatment.

And strangely enough, now that she was flat on her back in bed, with plenty of time, none of her excuses made any sense. Saving time for what? Work, work and more work. She'd buried herself in it, desperately afraid of the emotions she might have to face if she'd simply been still.

The door opened and she turned her head, the pillow cool against her cheek.

And there was Kevin, an impossibly big bouquet of roses in his hands. He set them down on her bedside table, then leaned over the bed and kissed her cheek.

"How are you?"

"So much better."

"I talked to the doctor. I had to know what was going on."

"It's okay."

They were silent for a minute, then Gillian said, "You were right. Nothing is worth this, let alone the job that I have."

"No, Gillie. It's not the job itself. You could be dancing and working yourself to death. You've got to reach a balance."

She knew he was going to say more, so she was silent.

"That first day, when we were getting ready to hit the road, I recognized where you were because I'd been there. I used to be in business for myself, and the work never stopped. I think part of the reason Jeane married me was because I came off as such a go-getter."

She reached for his hand and held on tightly.

"By the time I was thirty, I had two homes and was building a third. All the garages were filled with cars. Every night it was something, some charity here or a party there. Jeane loved it. But one day I was sitting in my office looking out the window." He took a deep breath, then met her eyes. "And I thought about the rest of my life stretched out in front of me, days and days of more of the same, and I knew I'd end up killing myself.''

He caught the look on her face and squeezed her hand.

"No, not that way. Not out the window. There are a lot more lethal ways to go, and mine was to stuff everything down and try to be what I thought everyone wanted me to be.

"I sold the house in Montana I was building in my spare time. Jeane had a fit when I stopped going to all the charity balls. We began to fight, but it felt good. And I knew that the only way I was going to get myself back was to destroy what had come before and start over.''

"When I told Jeane I wanted to sell the business, she went crazy. Kelly came to stay with us that weekend, she'd never liked Jeane to begin with, but I'd thought it was just some sister jealousy thing. She and Jeane got into it pretty bad, and Kelly accused her of being with me for what I could give her instead of loving me for who I was. When I heard that, I knew it was true. Once Kelly left, I told Jeane I wanted a divorce.''

"It was pretty ugly. I spent a lot of time talking with Gil and Lynne, trying to get it all straight in my head. I sold everything and ended up giving Jeane more than half just to get out. My cousin Ryan had heard about all of it from Kelly, and he offered me a job on one of his movies. It was an assistant-type thing. They were filming in the south of France and he thought getting out of the country and away from everything familiar might help me.

"And it did. I can't quite describe the way it happened, Gillie, but I can remember the day I started to feel alive again. Everyone was eating lunch, and I took a walk down this path and saw a bunch of ducks and all of a sudden I was just…happy. I hadn't been happy in a long time, and it took me a while to recognize it for what it was."

She nodded her head slowly, completely involved in his story. And she understood, because it had taken one Kevin MacClaine bursting into her life and rocking it to its foundation to make her feel anything.

"I'd had this life that was just *dead*. I woke up each morning and knew I had to put on a suit and go do things I didn't particularly like doing, knew I was going to be stuck in this rut for the rest of my life. And the worst thing was I could remember every decision that had gotten me there, and I'd sold myself out all the way.

"Even with Jeane. She was so different from any woman I'd ever known. If she was guilty for wanting me for what I could give her, then I was just as bad for wanting her on my arm.

"I kept in touch with Ryan, worked on a few more films. Eventually, I met Samantha. I used to watch her work with her animals and it fascinated me. And one night we were talking at their kitchen table and she asked me why I didn't consider working as a trainer myself."

He leaned back in the chair, his eyes still on Gillian's face. "And the rest is history."

She said nothing, simply squeezed his arm.

"I guess what I'm trying to say is that there's a part of your life that's yours alone, and if you don't have it, you don't have much of anything."

Her eyes filled then, as the emotional reality of what he was saying hit her full force.

"I know," she whispered.

KEVIN DROVE HER HOME from the hospital three days later. If he'd had had his way, he would have taken her straight to the compound, but Gillian asked him to give her time.

"Before I can be happy with you, I have to be happy with me. And right now I'm not so sure I am."

"I know exactly what you mean."

Her first day back at work she walked into Ben's office, shut the door, and told him she was leaving the firm.

"I'll miss you, Gillian," Ben said. But there was warmth in his eyes.

She nodded her head, not trusting herself to speak. This man had given her so much. Her first opportunity to stand on her own. Absolute faith that she could do so. A sense of pride and accomplishment in her work.

And Kevin.

"Just don't be a stranger," Ben said as he walked her to her office. "I've got your home number, and you have ours."

"I won't lose touch with you and Ashley."

Corbin came into her office as she was packing away the last of her things.

"Gillian?" He looked nervous as he stuck his blond head around the door. Ben had fired him the morning after the disastrous meeting, and he had returned only to pick up a few personal items.

"Come on in."

"Ben says you're leaving."

"Yep. It's time to recover."

Corbin had visited her in the hospital, looking like a scared little boy. And Gillian had seen it then, the differences between the two men. Where Kevin was strong, Corbin was weak. She'd never noticed it before because she'd never had that strong a contrast to hold up to her co-worker.

"I hope—you won't forget us all completely."

"I won't."

"I didn't mean for it to go as far as it did, Gillian. I just thought he was going to let the cat loose in a field or something. I didn't think he meant to seriously hurt Spike."

She had been putting the last of her things in a box, but now all movement stilled.

"Who meant to hurt him?"

Corbin couldn't meet her eyes. There were two spots of brilliant color in his pale cheeks. "MacKay's son, Tom. He was looking through the books and saw the kind of money MacClaine was making off Spike. He'd been cutting corners for the last year and a half, but he wanted more. And since the cat's contract was up for renegotiation, he thought he could replace him with one of his own."

"The Persian?"

"He bought it from a breeder. I met Tom at the Krunchies party, and we'd kept up a friendship of sorts. He came to me with the plan, and I—"

He stopped talking, and Gillian thought of all the myriad ways there were to sell out. How it could seem so easy.

"What did he do?"

"I got Spike out of the compound that night. MacClaine was picking up some supplies, he wasn't around. But then when we were driving back toward Tom's house—"

"Go on."

"He threw the cat out of the car."

"Oh, my God!"

"On the freeway. I tried to grab the cat, that's when I got the worst of the scratches. Don't—don't be too hard on MacClaine for losing his temper. I deserved it. Spike could have been killed, we were in the far left lane—"

"Oh, Corbin. Why did you go along with it at all?"

Now he was hanging his head, staring down at the carpet.

"You'd never understand, not in a million years, what it's like to be in a family where you don't quite measure up."

"You'd be surprised."

He didn't even hear her. "I've been trying to make Ben proud of me for years, and all he's ever noticed is you."

Gillian bit her lip against the automatic denial, because she knew it was true.

"I'll never measure up. I'll never be quite good enough. Don't think I don't know it. But I never wanted to take it out on you."

"I know. I know. Corbin, is there anything else you wanted to do? I mean, besides sit in an office and think up ad campaigns."

She saw the change in his face the minute the thought entered his mind.

"I always wanted— No, it was silly."

"Go on."

"I always wanted to buy a sailboat and sail around the world. Classic cliché, huh? But I always thought it would be wonderful to go new places and see new things."

"I wanted to be a dancer."

"You did?"

She nodded her head. "Somewhere along the line I lost my nerve. And it all wound up in my stomach." She thought for a second. "Corbin, you've got enough money to buy your boat."

"If I sold my Porsche. It's always breaking down, anyway. But . . . but I'm too old," said Corbin, the doubts returning.

"Grandma Moses started painting when she turned eighty," Gillian shot back.

"What if something happened—"

"Corbin. Listen to me. What if something never does? What if you stay locked in an office for the rest of your life and *nothing ever happens*?"

"What about your dancing?" he asked suddenly.

"I," she said, pulling herself up to her full height and feeling happier than she had in years, "am going back to class. Right after I leave, I'm buying myself a leotard and heading straight for a dance studio."

He had the funniest expression on his face, then before she knew what he meant to do, Corbin loped clumsily around her desk and gave her a quick hug.

"I'm going to do it. Oh, my God, I think I'm going to tell Linda tonight."

"Do it. Don't waste any more time."

She watched him as he left, then gathered her things. And as she took one last look at her office, she thought of how ironic it was that her final moments at the Merrill Advertising Agency had been her most creative.

THE DANCE STUDIO on Beverly Boulevard was like any other. The classrooms were upstairs, and as Gillian climbed each of those stairs, she felt like she was returning after a long journey.

"What kind of class are you interested in?" The woman who ran the school had to be past sixty, but her face was remarkably unlined, her dark hair pulled back in the classic dancer's knot.

"Ballet. Beginning. I took classes for years, but I stopped going a while ago."

"Why did you stop?" The woman seemed genuinely interested.

"I—"

I didn't have time.

Bryant needed me with him.

I wanted to be the best, but I didn't want to risk anything.

I was scared.

"I stopped believing in myself."

Those dark eyes were wise as they studied her. The woman slowly smiled, then said, "You missed it."

"Every day."

"There's a class in twenty minutes."

"I'll be there."

She'd bought leotards and tights on the way to the studio, and now she ran back down to her car, grabbed the bag and raced back up the stairs to the dressing room.

Another class had just ended, and the dressing room was flooded with young girls, chattering and giggling. Memories overwhelmed her, of another class, another time, another young girl.

She had to sit down on the bench when she started to undress because her hands were shaking.

I took a walk down this path and saw a bunch of ducks and all of a sudden I was just . . . happy.

Happy.

As she gathered up her tights and started to put them on, she wondered at the fact that it usually took so little to create happiness, but at the same time it took all the courage you possessed to believe you deserved it.

She was just finishing pulling on her leotard when she noticed the group of girls swarming by the bulletin board at the far end of the room. After stowing away her clothing in the locker provided, curiosity got the better of her and she walked over to the crowd.

Peering over the heads of the girls, she could just make out the list on the board. The smile started from deep inside as she read the familiar names.

Clara.

The Nutcracker.

The Sugarplum Fairy.

"Who's Lisa Cameron?"

"I am." The girl who answered was slender, with long blond hair and serious gray eyes.

"Congratulations." Gillian stuck out her hand, and Lisa, without any hesitation, accepted it.

"Thanks."

"It's a terrific part. It was always my favorite."

"Mine, too."

Then she walked swiftly past them, out into the studio where others were already at the barre, warming up. No matter where they were or how they differed, to a dancer a studio is always home.

And Gillian, grasping the barre and looking at herself in the long mirror, knew she'd finally come home.

"IT SOUNDS LIKE a great class."

"It is! And Kevin, you won't believe this! There's a woman I met, she's just one year younger than me, and she gets work in music videos all the time. It's more modern dance than ballet, but she said if I had a picture taken, once I was back in shape she'd let me know where the auditions were and I could try out."

"Michael Jackson's version of the Sugarplum Fairy. The industry won't know what's hit them." He laughed, and she loved the sound of that laugh, rich and full and warm. "I'm sure I can talk to Ryan and see if he knows if anyone needs a dancer."

"I don't know if I'd do it full time—"

"Why not?"

"Oh, Kevin, just to be dancing again—"

She went to classes every day, fell into the rhythm of using her body to its fullest capacity. Muscles she hadn't used in years began to ache, then respond. Gillian found herself waking up in the morning with a sense of adventure, of anticipation, that she hadn't had in years.

And Kevin. He was a solid presence in her life, and she'd never been happier. They dated steadily, saw each other twice a week, then three times, then five, then spent nights together at either the compound or her town house. She knew where the relationship was headed; it was like a long slow dive into the coolest, sweetest water ever.

He watched her all the time. Studied her. He seemed to want to put certain feelings into words, and one night out at dinner at their favorite Italian restaurant, she forestalled him.

"Just a little more time, Kevin. Please." Though she knew she loved him, there was something almost overwhelming about this man. He would never hurt her, she had no doubts about that, but she felt there were pieces of herself she had to pick up and put together before she could go to him with absolutely no hesitation.

She saw the flash of masculine impatience in his eyes, then he took her hand and squeezed it.

"I'm being selfish. It's just that I don't want to wait much longer. Give me some idea, Gillie, when you'll be ready."

"Just a little longer."

"You know what I'm going to ask you."

She nodded her head, her throat suddenly tight. How could she be scared of committing to this man after all they'd been through? After the way she knew she felt about him? Why was it that, for her, at this moment, love didn't seem to be enough?

"Am I going to lose you?" he asked softly.

"No. No. Kevin, I don't even understand it myself. But I promise you, it won't be much—"

"No pressure, Gillie. I'm sorry. It's no good at all if you don't come willingly." He smiled self-deprecatingly. "I forget all my instincts as a trainer when I'm around you."

His attempt to lighten up what was becoming a painful conversation brought quick tears to her eyes and a fresh surge of determination.

"June," Gillie said suddenly, forcing the words out of her mouth. "I'll be ready by the end of June."

"Hey, Gillie, why don't you come along?"

An audition. The idea terrified her.

"No, I don't think so." She turned her attention back to pulling on her tights, then her leotard. The dressing room and dance studio had become her second home, she was putting in more and more hours, spending more and more time there.

"Come on, it'll be fun!" Meg sat down next to her, her tousled honey-blond hair spilling over her slim shoulders, her green eyes twinkling. "What're you going to do, spend all your time hiding out in here and never going for the big time?"

"What kind of audition?"

"Modern dance. It's a video for that group, you know, the one with the lead singer who wrote the score for *Velvet Death*. The one we saw last week."

"Who are we supposed to be?"

"She's weakening," Meg yelled over her shoulder to Betsy, her usual audition partner. Both women seemed fearless to Gillie; Meg was all bubbly energy and Betsy was full of quiet determination. Gillie wasn't quite sure where she fit in.

Betsy, her dark hair pulled back with a ribbon, came up and leaned against one of the lockers. "What can it hurt, one audition? So they think you stink—there's three more later in the week."

They weren't going to let her get out of it this time. Yet Gillie still wanted to refuse.

"Bets, wait in the car for me, okay?" Meg said suddenly.

Once her friend was gone, Meg said, "I'm sorry. I shouldn't bully you into doing it. It's just that—when we first talked about it, you seemed interested."

"I was. I am."

"Then let's go."

Gillie looked into Meg's clear green eyes and marveled that there were people on the planet with such unbounded courage.

She couldn't meet that courage with anything but the truth.

"I just get scared."

"The funny thing is, you're better than Bets and me combined. I get scared, Gillie. I didn't even start dancing until I was thirteen. But you just have to do it. Don't think about it. Do it."

And Gillie remembered her conversation with Corbin and wondered at what an absolute hypocrite she was. If she didn't do this, she wouldn't be able to stand herself.

"Okay. I'm going. Let's go now."

"My car's parked in front. I just have to get some stuff out of my locker, it's so dirty it's beginning to dance by itself."

Gillie pulled on a large T-shirt and belted it into some semblance of a mini dress, then grabbed her large tote bag and headed down the stairs.

Meg was almost down those same stairs when the phone rang.

"Kevin? Hi! You just missed her. We're heading out for an audition—Gillie's first, I finally talked her into it. In about an hour, maybe two. It's that theater on Wilshire."

She gave him the address.

"I won't tell her we talked. What are you up to, Kevin?"

Meg was laughing when she hung up the phone.

"CLEMENTINE, WOULD YOU LIKE some tea?" Johanna's voice was quite proper, as befitted the hostess of a tea party.

And Birdy, sitting in one of the small chairs around the table outside, wondered how fate worked in finding her the perfect job.

Clementine was wearing a straw hat with flowers, and Spike was in another chair, a huge red bow around his neck.

"Would you like some tea, Spike?" Johanna poured water into the cat's teacup, then put some cat treats on the small plate in front of him. Spike, amazingly calm around small children, gazed at Johanna and then began to eat.

Kevin had built the playhouse, complete with front porch, on one of the corners of the compound. It was a well-loved little house, used by his nieces and nephews when they came to visit.

"Birdy, would you like some tea?"

She nodded, then let Johanna fill her cup. Birdy glanced up as movement caught her eye.

Kevin was running towards them. Once he reached them, he gave Johanna a hug and a kiss, politely declined her offer of tea, then turned his attention to Birdy.

"I'm going to be out this evening. Can you stay a little later and watch Johanna, until Sam gets here? It's important."

And Birdy smiled, knowing it had something to do with Gillian.

"Of course, I can. Don't worry, we'll be fine."

Kevin slanted an amused glance at Spike, eating his treats off the small table, and Clem, shaking her head and trying to dislodge the straw hat.

"I think I'll need Spike this afternoon, Johanna."

"Okay."

He picked up the large tabby, settling him up on his shoulder.

"Give my best to Gillian," Birdy said.

He grinned, winked and started on his way.

Men in love are wonderful to see, Birdy thought as she watched his retreating figure.

"Thanks," he called back, running toward the driveway and his Jeep.

And Birdy stared after him, her thoughts on another man, another courtship. And she was thankful she'd had her husband to love, and happy Kevin was going to have Gillian in his life.

They were good together, Kevin and Gillian, and she was sure they had a future. He was a kind man, giving her this job when she knew he really didn't need to employ anyone else at the compound. Letting her bring Michael out during the weekend.

And Johanna... She hadn't realized how much she missed her daughter until this little one had come into her life.

Clem grunted, and Birdy smiled as Johanna gave the pig another cookie.

"Not too many, dear."

"Just that one. Birdy, can I have you for a grandmother?"

Every time she thought Johanna had touched her, the child came up with something else.

"You have a grandmother, don't you?"

"She's in Boston. And she's not as much fun as you are. She's too old."

"I'm pretty old myself."

"No, you're not!"

"We'll have to ask your mother."

"She'll say yes. I can make her say yes."

This one was a real handful.

"All right."

"Good." And when Johanna smiled and those deep green eyes lit up, Birdy shook her head and knew Ryan and Sam were going to have some lively years ahead.

"YOU CAN WARM UP IN THIS ROOM. We'll be calling you shortly." The man with the clipboard was tall, blond and slender, with long, artistic fingers. Gillian smiled at him, even though her legs felt like lead and her hands were cold.

"Thanks."

They'd been given a brief overview of the video. Boy meets girl, boy loses girl, they dance together and

love triumphs over all. While the boy in this video—
the lead singer—wasn't going to have to dance much
except for some standard rock-and-roll moves, the girl
had to be a dancer. The singer wanted a particular
look as well as a woman who could perform the dance
routine his choreographer had painstakingly worked
out.

"I thought you said we were auditioning for part of
the chorus," Gillie whispered to Meg as she held on to
the barre and started to stretch.

"So I was wrong. Maybe that's the one at the end
of the week." But the green eyes sparkled, and Gillie
had to smile in spite of herself. She had a feeling Meg
knew exactly what she was doing.

All too soon her name was called.

Her hands shook as she stepped away from the
safety of the barre, and she felt Meg squeeze her arm.

"C'mon, Gillie. Blow 'em away."

They'd been briefed by the choreographer, shown
the steps, and had heard the song while warming up.
But now, up on the brightly lit stage in front of the
darkened theater, Gillie had never felt so completely
alone.

"Gillian Sommers?" a voice asked out of the darkness.

A bored voice.

She swallowed quickly, her throat dry. "Yes?"
What should have been a declaration came out as a
squeak.

Someone coughed. A paper rattled.

"Well, let's see it."

His attitude stung her, and quick anger filled her,
pushing away any fear. The music started, the beat

pulsing and intense, and the thoughts she'd had about this particular character rushed into her head.

Cocky. This woman would dance with a false bravado, because the most frightening thing in the world was to be vulnerable, in love.

But it was also the most liberating.

The months of classes, the hours of work, had turned her body into an instrument of passionate expression, and now Gillie could feel her anger turning into excitement.

She hadn't performed in a long time.

Convinced she didn't have a chance, and not even caring, she decided in the space of a heartbeat she would give them everything.

And after it was over, as the music faded and she pushed a tendril of hair out of her face, she wondered at the fact that once you took the first step, the rest was so very easy.

She liked that certain kind of silence that had fallen over the darkened theater, and she knew even if she never auditioned again in her life, she'd finally broken free.

Not waiting for their answer, she started to walk off the stage. Her body was humming, pulsing with happiness. This was what she had wanted to do all her life, and now—a little late—she finally had the courage to do it.

"Miss Sommers?"

The voice wasn't bored anymore.

She grinned into the darkness, shielding her eyes against the glare from the stagelights.

"Yes?" She sounded confident. Assured. Cocky.

"Do we have your picture and résumé?"

She nodded her head.

"Where have I seen you before?"

She couldn't resist the fib.

"Vegas."

"Ah." The voice accepted the fib. "How long have you been dancing?"

"All of my life." It wasn't really a lie, if she counted her dreams.

There was a pause, and she waited, knowing there was more.

"Could you come back next week?"

A rush of pure joy filled her. "What time?"

"Three would be fine."

"I'll be here."

Back at the barre, she told Meg and Betsy what had happened.

"I knew it!" Meg said. "Ah, Gillie, I'm glad you decided to come."

"Thanks for bugging me." She pushed her hair out of her eyes, then said, "I'll wait for you guys and we can get something to drink after."

"Walk outside with me," Meg said suddenly. "It's too hot in here."

Gillian wasn't even out the door when she saw Kevin. The Jeep was parked directly in front of the theater, in a green zone. He was leaning against it, a huge bouquet of red roses in his arms, and when he saw her he broke into a grin.

"What are you doing here?" she said breathlessly. She'd run down the stairs toward him, and now that she was standing in front of him, she felt suddenly shy.

"I think dancers usually get flowers." He held them out to her and she took them, burying her face in the soft petals and delicate fragrance.

"How did you know I was here?"

He nodded his head toward Meg, still standing at the top of the stairs.

"You're crazy," she said softly.

"I love you," he replied, never taking his eyes off her face.

She started to laugh. "Okay. Wait a minute, we have to do this again."

"Whatever you say."

She handed him the bouquet. "Stay right there."

And she ran back up the stairs until she was next to Meg.

"What're you doing up here when you've got a guy down there with *roses*?"

"Just go back inside a second. We're doing this over."

They walked back out again, and as soon as she saw Kevin, she raced down the stairs and jumped into his arms.

He caught her, crushing two of the roses and smashing the big red bow.

She kissed him, arms and legs wound tight around him, one of her hands in his hair. She couldn't stop kissing him, even when she felt the tears begin to slide down her cheeks.

When their lips finally parted, she buried her face against the warmth of his neck.

"Yes," she said softly.

The roses fell to the ground as he used his now free hand to tilt her chin so he could see her face.

"You're sure?" he said quietly.

"Yes. Oh, yes."

"Why, Gillie," he said, grinning that heart-stopping grin she loved, "and it's not even June."

"I guess I'm just feeling frisky. Let's do it."

"Why, Miss Sommers—"

"Not that. Let's go to Vegas."

"Now?" She'd caught him off guard and it delighted her.

"Now."

"Meow."

"What was that?" she said, then saw Spike in the back seat, a bedraggled bow around his neck. He was stretching, as if just waking up from a nap.

"What's he doing here?" she asked.

"I figured it this way. He was the one who brought us together, I thought he should be in on the big moment."

"You were going to ask me."

"I'm an impatient man, Gillie. Can you live with that?"

"Sure." She picked Spike up, and gently wiggled the bow free.

"I'll call Samantha and see if she can do the next few feedings."

"You really want to?"

He kissed her. "Why waste time?"

Why indeed.

"Almost there," Kevin said softly.

Gillian blinked, then sat up in her seat. Evening had fallen over the desert, but on the horizon she could make out the Vegas Strip, the lights glittering in the distance.

"Last chance to back out," he teased.

"Not a chance. You're stuck with me."

He reached over and held her hand, and Gillie felt suddenly as if everything good in life were stretched out ahead of her, to be discovered with this man.

Spike yawned, and she looked down at the cat in her lap.

He blinked up at her sleepily, and then...she could have sworn that he winked.

She scratched his head and he began to purr, a deep, rumbling sound.

I owe you one, Green Eyes.

H A R L E Q U I N
American Romance®

COMING NEXT MONTH

#341 IMAGINE by Anne McAllister

Frances Moon was a woman of the '90s. The 1890s, that is. At least she was convinced she'd have been more comfortable back then. She had everything she needed in the wilds of Vermont. And if she'd wanted a man, she could create one. Then Jack Neillands showed up. Inch-for-masculine-inch he embodied her perfect man. But fantasy heroes were safe and predictable . . . and Jack was anything but!

#342 LUCKY PENNY by Judith Arnold

Syndicated columnist Jodie Posniak got all sorts of household hints, recipes and questions from her readers. Until now she'd never gotten a love letter. Into Tom Barrett's missive, Jodie read an aching over lost love. Though his words were simple, she envisioned a man who would charm her with his tenderness . . . and ignite her with his passion.

#343 SPIRITS WILLING by Leigh Ann Williams

New Yorker Angie Sullivan flew off to the Coast to collaborate with a Hollywood living legend on her autobiography and found her employer distracted by a New Age mystic who'd spellbound Tinseltown. Angie suspected she was being hoodwinked California-style. Angie's own mental energy was being diverted by guru biographer Lance Wright, who definitely enhanced Angie's aura—on a purely sensual plane.

#344 BEST BEHAVIOR by Jackie Weger

Willa Manning longed to give her beloved adopted daughter the grandparents she dreamed of, but not at the risk of losing her forever. Nicholas Cavenaugh understood Willa's reservations, but he'd promised to bring his friends the child their lost daughter had borne so far from home. Fate, which had brought Nicholas and Willa together, had put them on opposite sides in the only struggle that could tear them apart.

**In April, Harlequin brings you the
world's most popular romance author**

JANET DAILEY

No Quarter Asked

Out of print since 1974!

After the tragic death of her father, Stacy's world is shattered. She
needs to get away by herself to sort things out. She leaves behind
her boyfriend, Carter Price, who wants to marry her. However, as
soon as she arrives at her rented cabin in Texas, Cord Harris, owner
of a large ranch, seems determined to get her to leave. When Stacy
has a fall and is injured, Cord reluctantly takes her to his own ranch.
Unknown to Stacy, Carter's father has written to Cord and asked
him to keep an eye on Stacy and try to convince her to return home.
After a few weeks there, in spite of Cord's hateful treatment that
involves her working as a ranch hand and the return of Lydia, his ex-
fiancée, by the time Carter comes to escort her back, Stacy knows
that she is in love with Cord and doesn't want to go.

**Watch for *Fiesta San Antonio* in July and
For Bitter or Worse in September.**

Have You Ever Wondered If You Could Write A Harlequin Novel?

Here's great news—Harlequin is offering a series of cassette tapes to help you do just that. Written by Harlequin editors, these tapes give practical advice on how to make your characters—and your story— come alive. There's a tape for each contemporary romance series Harlequin publishes.

Mail order only

All sales final

TO: ***Harlequin Reader Service***
Audiocassette Tape Offer
P.O. Box 1396
Buffalo, NY   14269-1396

I enclose a check/money order payable to HARLEQUIN READER SERVICE® for $9.70 ($8.95 plus 75¢ postage and handling) for EACH tape ordered for the total sum of $_____*
Please send:

[Romance and Presents   [Intrigue
    American Romance   Temptation
    Superromance   All five tapes ($38.80 total)

Signature_____
Name·_____
(please print clearly)
Address _____
State _____ Zip·_____

*Iowa and New York residents add appropriate sales tax

AUDIO-H